Elias Portolu

»»»»»»»»» «««««««««

Grazia Deledda

ELIAS
PORTOLU

TRANSLATED FROM THE ITALIAN BY
MARTHA KING

NORTHWESTERN UNIVERSITY PRESS

EVANSTON, ILLINOIS

»»»»»»»»»» «««««««««

Northwestern University Press
Evanston, Illinois 60208-4210

Printed in the United States of America

ISBN 0-8101-1250-7 cloth
ISBN 0-8101-1251-5 paper

The paper used in this publication meets the minimum requirements of the
American National Standard for Information Sciences—Permanence of Paper
for Printed Library Materials, ANSI Z39.48-1984.

GLOSSARY

cattas	A kind of fritter of raised dough, made with eggs, milk and *aquavite*
filindeu	Thick cheese soup that can be eaten cold
foccacce	A flat bread, often seasoned with oil and salt
focolare	Four stones placed on the floor in the middle of the room, on which a fire is made for cooking. As there is no chimney, the smoke must find its way out through the roof
fritelle	Little cakes
gattos	A Nuorese cake made of almonds, sugar and honey
novena	A Roman Catholic devotion consisting of special prayers or services on nine successive days
sapa	A kind of boiled wine
seranu	The people's masked ball
sudarium	A napkin or cloth for wiping the face in Rome
tanca	A large expanse of enclosed land for pasturing sheep, cows, pigs
Zio, Zia	Literally, 'uncle', 'aunt': a common appellative of respect for older people

I

Happy days were coming for the Portolu family of Nuoro. At the end of April their son Elias, who had served his time in a penitentiary on the continent, would come home; then Pietro, the older of the three Portolu boys, was to be married.

They were preparing for some kind of festival: the house was freshly whitewashed, the wine and the bread[1] were ready; it seemed that Elias would return to his studies and - his disgrace over and done with - his relatives were waiting for him with a certain pride.

The long-awaited day finally arrived. Especially eager was his mother, Zia Annedda, a placid little whitehaired woman, slightly deaf, who loved Elias more than her other two sons. Pietro, who was a farmer, Mattia and Zio Berte (their father), who were shepherds, came back from the countryside.

The two brothers Pietro and Mattia closely

resembled one another: short, robust, bearded, with bronze faces and long black hair. Zio Berte Portolu (the old fox, as they called him) was also short, with black tangled hair that fell to his sick red eyes and grew over his ears to mingle with his long black beard, no less tangled. He was wearing a rather dirty costume,[2] with a long black sleeveless overjacket of sheepskin, the wool turned inside; and within all that black fur one saw only two enormous reddish bronze hands, and a huge nose the same reddish bronze protruding from his face.

However, for the solemn occasion, Zio Portolu had washed his hands and face; requesting a little olive oil from Zia Annedda, he oiled his hair well, then he untangled it with a wooden comb, exclaiming loudly from the pain that this operation caused him.

'May the devil comb you,' he said to his hair, twisting his head. 'Sheep's wool isn't this tangled!'

When the knots were untangled, Zio Portolu began making a little braid over his right temple and another over the left, a third under his right ear, a fourth under his left ear. Then he oiled and combed his beard.

'Now make two more of them!' laughed Pietro.

'Don't I look like a groom?' shouted Zio Portolu. And he laughed too. He had a characteristic, forced laugh that didn't move a hair on his beard.

Zia Annedda muttered something because she didn't like her sons to be disrespectful to their father; but he looked at her reproachfully and said: 'Well, what's wrong with that? Let the boys laugh; it's their time to enjoy themselves; we've already had our fun.'

Meanwhile the time for Elias' arrival drew near. Some relatives came and a brother of Pietro's fiancée, and they all set off for the station. Zia Annedda stayed home alone, with the cat and the chickens.

The little house, with an inner courtyard, faced a steep path that descended to the main road. Beyond the wall skirted by the path were some gardens overlooking the valley. It seemed out in the country: a tree stretched its branches over a bush, giving the path a picturesque air. Granite Mount Orthobene and Oliena's blue mountains blocked the horizon.

Zia Annedda was born and had grown old there, in that little corner full of pure air, and perhaps for that reason had always remained as simple and pure as a seven-year-old. Moreover, the whole neighbourhood was inhabited by decent people, by girls who went to church, by families with simple ways.

Zia Annedda went out of the open front door every once in a while, looked here and there, and then went back in. Even the neighbours were waiting for the prisoner's homecoming, standing by their little doors or sitting on the rough stone benches against the wall. Aunt Annedda's cat gazed from the window.

And then the sound of voices and footsteps in the distance. A neighbour hurried across the path and stuck her head inside Aunt Annedda's door.

'They're here!' she shouted.

The little woman went outside, trembling and paler than usual; immediately afterwards a group of townspeople burst on to the path, and Elias, overcome by emotion, ran to his mother and took her in his arms.

'A hundred years before another misfortune, a hundred years before another . . .'[3] Zia Annedda murmured through her tears.

Elias was tall and thin, with a very white, delicate, clean-shaven face; he had short-clipped black hair, his eyes were blue-green. The long imprisonment had left his hands and face white.

All the neighbours crowded around him, pushing the other townspeople away, and they shook his hand, wishing him: 'A hundred years before another misfortune.'

'God willing!' he replied.

After that they went into the house. The cat, who had retreated from the window at the approach of the townspeople, jumped off the outside stairs in fright, ran around here and there, then went into hiding.

'*Musci, musci*,'[4] Zio Portolu began to shout, 'what's got into you, haven't you ever seen people before? Oh, are we assassins that even cats run from? We are honest, we are honourable people!'

The old fox had a great need to shout, to chatter, and he was talking nonsense.

Everyone sat in the kitchen while Zia Annedda poured something to drink, and Zio Portolu took possession of Jacu Farre, one of his relatives – a handsome man, ruddy and plump, who breathed heavily – and didn't leave him in peace.

'Look,' he shouted at him, tugging at his coat tails

4

and motioning toward his sons. 'See my three sons now? Three doves! And strong, eh, and healthy, and handsome! See them standing there in a row, see them? Now that Elias is back we are like four lions; not even a fly can touch us. I'm strong, too, you know; don't look at me like that, Jacu Farre, I don't give a damn, understand? My son Mattia is my right hand; now Elias will be my left. And then Pietro, little Pietro, Prededdu mio. See him? He's a marvel! He's sown ten measures of barley and eight of wheat and two measures of beans. Eh, if he wants to get married, he can take good care of a wife! He'll have a good harvest. He's a marvel, Prededdu mio. Ah, my sons! No one in Nuoro has sons like mine.'

'Eh! Eh!' the other one said, almost moaning.

'Eh! Eh! What do you mean with your eh! eh!, Jacu Fà? That I'm lying, maybe? Show me another three young men like my honest, hardworking, strong sons. They are real men, they are!'

'Did anyone tell you they're women?'

'Women, women! You'll be a woman, barrel-belly,' shouted Zio Portolu, pushing on the stomach of his relative with his two large hands. 'You, not them, my sons! Don't you see them?' he continued, turning in adoration towards the three young men. 'Don't you see them? Are you blind? Three doves . . .'

Zia Annedda came over with a glass in one hand and a carafe in the other. She filled the glass and handed it to Farre, and Farre courteously gave it to Zio Portolu. Zio Portolu drank it.

'Let's drink!⁵ To everyone's health! And you, my

wife, my little woman, never fear anything again. We are like lions, now, not even a fly can touch us.'

'Go along with you!' she answered.

She poured a drink for Farre and moved on. Zio Portolu followed her with his eyes. Then tapping his right ear, he said: 'She's a little . . . here; she doesn't hear well, after all, but a woman! A good woman! She minds her own business, my wife, she certainly minds her own business! And a conscientious woman, too! Ah, there's none other like her . . .'

'None other like her in Nuoro!'

'So it seems!' shouted Zio Portolu. 'Has anyone heard her gossip? Don't think that if Pietro brings his wife here she won't be well off, that girl!'

And soon he began to praise the young woman too. A rose, a jewel, a prize! She sewed and weaved, she was a good housekeeper, honest, beautiful, good, well-off.

'In conclusion,' said Farre sarcastically, 'there's none other like her in Nuoro!'

All this time the group of young men were talking eagerly with Elias, drinking, laughing, spitting. The one who laughed the most was the one who had returned home, but his laugh was weary and broken, his voice weak; his face and hands stood out among all those bronze faces and hands; he seemed like a woman dressed like a man. Besides, his speech had acquired something different, exotic; he spoke with a certain affectation, half Italian and half dialect, with curses wholly continental.

'Listen to your father brag about all of you,' Pietro's

6

future brother-in-law said. 'He says you are all doves, and truthfully you are white like a dove, Elias Portolu.'

'But you'll get dark again,' said Mattia. 'Tomorrow we'll start the ride to the sheepfold, isn't that right, my brother?'

'Whether he's white or black doesn't matter,' Pietro said. 'Let's stop this foolishness. Let him go on with what he was saying.'

'Well then, I was saying,' Elias took up where he had left off, with his weary voice, 'that grand gentleman, my cellmate, had been the chief of thieves in that big city that is called . . . I don't remember any more, oh well. He was with me, he confided everything. That one, yes, who they said was a thief. What did our thieving amount to? Over here we need something one day so we go out, steal a cow and sell it; they catch us and sentence us, and that cow isn't enough to pay a lawyer. But the men in there, those big thieves, are something else! They take millions, hide them, and when they get out of prison they're rich, they drive around in carriages and enjoy themselves. What are we Sardinian mules compared to them?'

The young men listened intently, full of admiration for those great thieves over the sea.

'Then there was even a monsignor,' continued Elias, 'a rich man who had thousands of lire in his bank account.'

'Even a monsignor! . . .' exclaimed Mattia in amazement.

Pietro looked at him smugly, wanting to appear nonchalant, even though he too was astonished.

7

'And so, a monsignor? Well, aren't monsignors men like the others? Prisons are built for men.'

'Why was he there?'

'Oh . . . because it seems he wanted to get rid of the king and put the pope in his place. However, others said that he, too, was in gaol for some kind of money business. He was a tall man with hair white as snow; he was always reading. Another died and left all the money he had in the bank to the inmates. They wanted to give me five lire; I refused it, though. A Sardinian doesn't take charity.'

'Stupid! I would have taken it!' shouted Mattia. 'I would have got blind drunk drinking to the health of the dead man.'

'It's not allowed,' replied Elias; and he stood a moment in silence, absorbed in vague memories, then exclaimed, 'Jesus! Jesus! How many people there were, every kind of person! There was another Sardinian with me, a marshal; they put him on board at Cagliari the same night they put me on. He thought they would let him go free, but instead they took him before he knew what was happening.'

'Oh, I'd have known!'

'Oh, I would too!'

'He bragged that they would soon pardon him, that he was a relative of the minister and that he had another relative at the king's court. But he was still there when I left; no one wrote to him, no one sent him a penny. And in *those places* if you don't have any money you die of hunger. God help me! And the gaolers!' he exclaimed, pulling a wry face, 'just so many tyrants! They're almost all Neapolitans, bullies; if they see you're dying they spit on you. But before I went away I said to one of them: "Try coming our way and I'll break your neck."'

'Yes,' said Mattia, 'try to get near our sheepfold and we'll give him something he won't forget!'

'Oh, he won't come this way!'

'Who won't?' asked Zio Portolu, coming over to them.

'A guard who spat on Elias,' said Mattia.

'No, devil, he didn't spit on me at all. What are you saying?'

Everyone began to laugh. Zio Portolu shouted: 'Elias wouldn't have allowed it. He would have broken his teeth with one blow. Elias is a man. We are men, we are, we aren't puppets made of fresh cheese like the continentals, even if they are the gaolers of men . . .'

'What do you mean, gaolers!' said Elias, lifting his shoulders. 'The gaolers are bullies; but there are gentlemen there; you should have seen them! Grand gentlemen who ride in carriages, who have thousands and thousands of lire in the bank when they go to prison.'

Zio Portolu got angry, spat, and said: 'What are they? Men made of fresh cheese! Get them to lasso a wild pony, or catch a bull, or fire an arquebus! They would die of fright first. What are gentlemen? My sheep are more courageous, so God help me.'

'And yet, and yet . . .' Elias insisted, 'if you could see . . .'

9

'What have you seen?' Zio Portolu retorted scornfully. 'You haven't seen anything. At your age I hadn't seen anything; but I saw things later and I know what gentlemen are, and what continentals are, and what Sardinians are. You're a little chick barely hatched out of the egg . . .'

'Anything but a chick!' Elias murmured, smiling bitterly.

'A rooster, then!' Mattia said.

And Farre, shrewdly: 'No, a little bird . . .'

'Escaped from its cage!' exclaimed the others, laughing.

The conversation became more general. Elias kept on recounting his memories, more or less exact, about the place and the people he had left. The others made comments and laughed. Zia Annedda was also listening, with a placid smile on her calm face, not hearing all of Elias' words very well; but Farre, sitting next to her, bent close and repeated out loud what he said.

In the meanwhile other people came – friends, neighbours, relatives. The newcomers went over to Elias, many kissed him , all wished him well.

'One hundred years before another.'

'God willing!' he responded, pulling his cap over his forehead.

And Zia Annedda poured them something to drink. Soon the kitchen was full of people; Zio Portolu shouted incessantly, letting everyone know that his sons were three doves, and he would like to keep everyone there a long time; but Pietro was anxious to

10

introduce Elias to his fiancée, and insisted on his going out with him.

'We're going out to get some air,' he said. 'This poor devil has been shut in because you want to keep him here all evening.'

'Some air will do him good!' said a relative. 'His face like a girl's will get black as gunpowder.'

'I'm sure of it!' shouted Elias, passing his hands over his face, ashamed of his whiteness.

But Pietro finally made himself understood, and they were getting ready to leave when his future mother-in-law came in, a thin widow, stiff and tall, with her pale face wrapped in a black veil. Her two younger children were with her, a girl and an arrogant young boy.

'My son!' the widow exclaimed rushing towards Elias with her arms open. 'May the Lord give you a hundred years before another misfortune like that one.'

'God willing!'

Zia Annedda went solicitously behind the widow, wanting to make her comfortable; but Zio Portolu took charge of the woman, taking hold of her hands and giving her a shake.

'See him?' he shouted in her face. 'See him, Arrita Scada? The dove has come back to its nest. Who can hurt us now? Who can hurt us? You say it, Arrita Scada . . .'

She didn't know how to reply.

'Let him talk,' exclaimed Pietro, turning to the widow. 'He's happy today.'

11

'Because he should be happy!'

'Certainly I'm happy. What are you saying? Shouldn't I be happy? Don't you see the dove? He's come back to the nest. He's as white as a lily. He knows some good stories to tell now. Arrita Scada, have you heard? We're a family, a house of men, we are. And tell your daughter that she's marrying a wonderful man, not rubbish.'

'I'm sure of it.'

'Do you believe it? Or do you think your daughter's coming here to be a maid? She'll be a lady, and she'll find bread, she'll find wine, she'll find corn, barley, beans, oil; all God's good things. You see that door?' he shouted then, making Zia Arrita turn towards a small door at the end of the kitchen. 'See it? Yes? Well, you know what's behind that door? One hundred *scudi* worth of cheese. And other things, too.'

'Stop it, stop it,' said Pietro, a little chagrined. 'She doesn't know what to make of your goods from God.'

'Besides,' observed Elias, 'Maria Maddalena Scada isn't marrying Pietro for our cheese.'

'My dear heart! Everything in the world is good!' exclaimed Zia Arrita, sitting down between her children. Her boy didn't speak, but smiled scornfully.

'Come on, come on, stop it!' Pietro repeated.

In the meanwhile Zia Annedda, seeing that they wouldn't let her say a word, began to make coffee[6] for her son's future mother-in-law.

'My husband,' she said as soon as she could have her all to herself, 'is too attached to the things of this world. He never thinks that the Lord has given us

12

these things, without our deserving them, and that the Lord can take them away from one minute to the next.'

'Annedda, my dear, all men are like that,' said the other woman to comfort her. 'They only think about the things of this world. Let's think no more of it. What are you doing? Don't go to any trouble. I've just come for a moment and I'm leaving straightaway. I see that Elias is well, he's as white as a girl, God bless him.'

'Yes, he seems to be all right, thank the Lord. He has suffered so much, poor little bird!'

'Ah, let's hope that's all finished. He surely won't go back to his bad companions, because it was his bad companions who got him into trouble.'

'Bless you. Your words are golden, my Arrita Scada. But what were we saying? Men think only about things of this world. If they would think just a little about the other world, they would go straighter in this one. They think this earthly life will never end; but it's a novena, this life, a novena and short as well. We suffer in this world; we do so so that this little bird here,' she touched her breast, 'is calm and free of guilt; let the rest go as it likes. Take some sugar, Arrita; watch out that your coffee isn't too bitter.'

'It's all right as it is; I don't like it sweet.'

'Well, we were saying that it's enough to have a clear conscience. Men don't pay attention to that. For them it's enough that the crop is good, that they get a lot of cheese, wheat and olives. Ah, they don't know that life is so short, that everything in this world passes

13

so quickly. Give me your cup, don't trouble yourself. Ah, it's nothing, I dropped the spoon. Things of the world! Go, Arrita Scada, go to the edge of the sea and count all the grains of the sand. When you have counted them you will know that they are nothing in comparison to the years of eternity. Yet, our years, the years we spend in this world, would fit inside a baby's fist. I always say these things to Berte Portolu and to all my sons; but they are too attached to the world.'

'They are young, my dear Annedda, you have to remember that, they are young. Besides, you will see that Elias has settled down; he's serious, very serious. It hasn't been an easy lesson, and it will serve him for the rest of his life.'

'May Maria di Valverde grant it! Ah, Elias is a kind-hearted young man; when he was a boy he seemed like a little girl; he didn't swear, never said a bad word. Whoever would have thought he would have made me shed so many tears?'

'Enough, now it's all in the past. Now your sons really seem like doves, like your husband Berte says. It's enough that they always get along, love one another . . .'

'Ah, that's in no danger, bless you!' said Zia Annedda smiling.

After dinner Zia Annedda finally found herself alone with Elias, both sitting outside in the courtyard. The front door was open, the lane deserted. It was like a summer's night, silent, with a transparent sky blooming with bright, clear stars. Beyond the gardens, beyond the road, far away, the silvery bell of a grazing sheep was heard; the sharp odour of fresh grass was in the air. Elias breathed that odour, that pure air, with dilated nostrils, with instinctive wild pleasure. He felt his blood running hot in his veins, and his head pleasantly heavy. He had had much to drink and he felt happy.

'We went to see Pietro's fiancée,' he said in a faraway voice, 'she's a very pretty girl.'

'Yes, she's dark, but pretty. She's smart enough besides.'

'Her mother seems a little arrogant to me. If she had a sixpence she'd pretend it was a shilling; but the girl seems unpretentious.'

'What do you expect? Arrita Scada comes from good stock and pride comes from that. Besides,' said Zia Annedda, entering into her favourite discussion, 'I don't know what one gets from arrogance and pride. God said: "Three things only are necessary to man: love, charity and humility." What does one get out of the other passions? You, now, have experienced life, my son; what do you say about it?'

Elias took a deep breath; he looked up at the sky.

'You're right; I've experienced life; not that I deserved the misfortune I had, because, you know, I was innocent, but because the Lord's ways are slow but sure. I've been a bad son, and God punished me. He's made me old before my time. Bad companions led me astray, and it's because I went around with them that I got mixed up in that trouble.'

'And while you were suffering those companions never even asked about you. Before, when you were free, they didn't leave that door over there in peace: "Where's Elias? Where's Elias?" Elias would go and Elias would come back. And afterwards? Afterwards they stayed away, or if they had to pass this way, they pulled their caps down over their foreheads so we wouldn't recognize them.'

'Enough! Now, it's all over; I'm starting a new life,' he said, sighing again. 'Now only my family exists for me: you, my father, my brothers. Ah, believe me, I'll make you forget all the past. I'll be like a servant, at your service, and it'll be as if I had been born again.'

Zia Annedda felt tears of sweetness rise to her eyes and, since it seemed to her that Elias was also moved too much, she changed the subject.

'Were you always well?' she asked. 'You've lost a lot of weight.'

'What could I do? In those places you lose weight without getting ill. Not working kills faster than any hard work.'

'You never worked?'

'Yes, they gave us some silly manual job, fit for a shoemaker or a woman! And so it seemed as if time never passed. One minute seemed like a year. It's been terrible, mamma.'

They were silent. Elias' voice had deepened as he said those last words. During the afternoon, in the first intoxication of freedom, he had spoken easily about his imprisonment and about his companions in misfortune, it already seeming a distant thing, almost

16

pleasant to recall. But now, in that silent darkness, smelling the fresh country smells that reminded him of the happy days of his early youth spent in the sheepfold, in the boundless freedom of his father's *tanca*, here with his mother, that good, pure, little old woman, the memory of years uselessly lost in the anguish of the penitentiary suddenly aroused a horror.

'I'm very weak,' he said after some minutes, 'I don't have the strength for anything. It's as though they've broken my back. And yet I was never ill; only once I had terrible colic, and I felt as if I was dying. *Santu Franziscu meu*, I said then, let me get out of this horror, and the first thing I'll do when I'm free will be to go to your church and light a candle.'

'*Santu Franziscu bellu!*' exclaimed Zia Annedda, clasping her hands. 'We'll go, we'll go there, my son! Bless you, you'll get your strength back, don't doubt it. We'll go and make the novena at St Francis' church. Pietro will come to the feast and bring his fiancée on his horse.'

'When's Pietro getting married?'

'After the harvest, my son.'

'He'll bring his bride here?'

'Yes, he'll bring her here, at least at first; I'm beginning to get old, my son, and I need help. As long as I live I want us all to be together. Afterwards, when I return to the bosom of the Lord, you can go your own ways. You'll marry too . . .'

'Oh, and who wants me?' he said bitterly.

'Why talk like that, Elias? Who wants you? A daughter of God. If you make amends, if you live an

17

honest, God-fearing, hard-working life, you'll have good fortune. I'm not saying you should look for a rich woman; but you'll find an honest woman. The Lord gave us matrimony to unite a man and a woman in a holy way, not only a rich man with a rich woman or a poor man with a poor woman.'

'Now, now!' he said with a laugh. 'Let's not talk about that! I just came back today, and we're already talking about marriage. We'll talk about it another day. I'm only twenty-three years old, and there's time. But you're tired, mamma. Go on, get some rest. Go.'

'I'm going; but you go to bed, too, Elias. The air could make you ill.'

'Ill?' he said, opening his mouth and breathing deeply. 'How can it make me ill? Don't you see that it gives me back life? Go on. I'll come in right away.'

After a moment he was alone, half-lying on the ground, with his elbow leaning on the doorstep. He heard his mother go up the wooden ladder, close the window, and take off her shoes. Then all was silent. The air was cool, almost humid, aromatic. He thought over the things his mother had said to him. Then he said to himself: 'My father and my brothers are sleeping peacefully on their mats. I can hear them from here. My father is snoring, Mattia is talking in his sleep from time to time; he is certainly dreaming, and even in his dreams he is a little simple. But how well they sleep! They are drunk, but tomorrow they won't feel a thing. I'm a little drunk, too, but I'll feel the effects. How weak I am! I'm no longer a man. I'll be good for nothing now. Oh, and my mother wants me to get married! But what woman wants me? None. Enough, the air is getting damp; time to go inside.'

But he didn't move. The tinkling of the grazing herds continued, seeming sometimes near, other times far away, carried by the humid, fragrant breeze. Elias felt tired, with a heavy head, and couldn't move, or it seemed he couldn't move. Confused visions began to weave in his imagination. He had always remembered the sheepfold, the *tanca* covered with tall hay, and now he saw the sheep with long fleece, scattered here and there in the green pasture; but these sheep had human faces, the faces, that is, of his companions in misfortune. He felt an undefinable anxiety. Perhaps the wine fermenting in his blood was giving him a little fever. He remembered the events of the day, but he seemed to have dreamed them, and now he found himself in *that place* feeling dark pain.

The fantastic images of his dream undulated, faded, disappeared. Now it seemed that those strange sheep with human faces were jumping over the wall enclosing the *tanca*; he followed behind them anxiously, also jumping over the wall and entering the adjoining *tanca*, thick with tall, deep-green cork trees. A big, tall, rigid man with a reddish-grey beard, a kind of giant, was walking slowly, almost majestically, through the woods. Elias recognized him immediately: he was a man from Orune, a primitive wise man who watched over the immense *tanca* of a property owner from Nuoro, so no one would steal the cork. From the time he was a boy Elias had known this gigantic man who never laughed, and perhaps for that reason enjoyed a

19

certain reputation as a sage. His name was Martinu Monne, but everyone called him the Father of the Woods because he would tell that, after his childhood, he had not slept a single night in town.

'Where are you going?' he asked Elias.

'I'm following these crazy sheep. But I'm so tired, my Father of the Woods! I can't take any more; I'm weak and undone; I'm not worth anything.'

'Eh, if you don't want any bother, be a priest!' said Zio Martinu in his powerful voice.

'Eh, eh, that idea occurred to me more than once in *that place*!' Elias shouted.

He shook himself, and woke up with a cold shiver.

'I've gone to sleep here,' he thought as he got up. 'I'm liable to catch something.'

He entered the kitchen staggering a bit. His father and brothers were sleeping heavily on their mats; a lamp placed on the *focolare* stones was burning. For Elias, poor thing, in such a weakened condition, a bed was made up in a little bedroom on the ground floor. He took the lamp, crossed through a little room where there was a large quantity of yellow, oily, unpleasant smelling cheese on wide tables, and went into the little bedroom.

He took off his clothes, lay down and put out the lamp. It felt as if his back was broken, his head heavy. And yet he could not go to sleep, again oppressed by troubled drowsiness, full of confused dreams. He saw the *tanca* again, the hay, the sheep fat with tangled yellow wool, the green line of the neighbouring woods.

20

Zio Martinu was still there; but now he was next to the wall, tall, rigid, dirty, majestic.

He too was standing next to the wall, by their *tanca*. Elias was telling him many things about *that place*. Among other things he was saying: 'They always took us to mass, they made us go to confession and communion often. Ah, down there we're good Christians. The chaplain was a saintly man. I once told him, in confession, that I had gone as far as high school, and then I had become a shepherd, but that many times I had regretted not going on with my studies. Then he gave me a book, one side in Latin and the other in Italian, the book of the Seventh Saint. I've read it more than a hundred – what am I saying? – more than a thousand times. I've brought it here, too. I know how to read in Latin as well as in Italian.'

'Then you are a very wise person!'

'Not as wise as you! I'm afraid of God, though.'

'Well, when a man fears God he is wiser than kings,' said Zio Martinu.

Here Elias' dream mixed and blended with other dreams more or less as strange.

II

Although Mattia wanted Elias to go to the sheepfold with him right away, he stayed at home for several days, receiving visits from friends and relatives, and just resting.

Zio Berte and Mattia went back to the sheepfold, Pietro to his work; but one or the other would come back to town in the evening to see Elias and keep him company. Then there would be much talk and stories around the *focolare* or in the courtyard on the clear spring evenings. Elias didn't undergo the police surveillance that now usually follows and aggravates the pain;[7] but the police kept an eye on him, at least for the first few days; and often in the evening two *carabinieri* would come up the lane with heavy steps, stop, and stick their heads inside Zio Berte's front door.

If Zio Berte was in the house and caught sight of the *carabinieri* with his little sick fox eyes, he would get up in his half-respectful and half-mocking manner, and go to the door to invite them in.

'Welcome to the king, welcome to the police!' he would shout. 'Come on in, here young men, come drink a glass of wine. Oh, you don't want to come in? Oh, do you think this is a house of assassins or thieves? We are honourable men and you don't have to stick your nose in our business.'

Those two ruddy, fat young men would deign to smile.

'Are you coming in or not?' Zio Portolu would go on. 'Shall I drag you in? Do you want me to drag you in? Watch out or part of you will come off in my hand. If you don't want to come in go to the devil. Zio Portolu has good wine!'

Finally they would come in. And soon Zia Annedda would be there with the famous carafe.

'Long live the king, long live power, long live wine! Drink, that justice may be dealt you . . .'

'Oh, oh,' Mattia would observe if he were there, 'what are you saying, my papa! They deal it out themselves.'[8]

'Ha, ha, ha!'

'There's nothing to laugh about. Drink, my boys. And you drink too, Mattia, because it's good for your head. And you too, Elias, who have a face the colour of ashes. Men should be ruddy. You see these young men? You should be ruddy like them. All right then, you two are getting even redder in the face, what the devil! Zio Portolu's words embarrass you, perhaps? Eh, he has made others besides you blush! He has

23

made dragoons blush, Zio Portolu has. You don't know who Zio Portolu is? Well, I'll tell you. I am he.'

'A pleasure!' the two young men would say, bowing and laughing. They would enjoy themselves, and Zio Portolu's wine was truly good – sparkling and aromatic.

Zio Berte would allow himself the liberty of putting his hands on the *carabinieri*.

'What do you think, you, the powerful ones! Nonsense! If I take this long knife, this pistol and these buttons off you, what's left? Nothing, I tell you. Let's put these things on my Elias, Mattia and Pietro. Here they are, better than you. Three flowers, three doves. My sons! You don't have to say anything to my sons. They don't need to steal, because we have enough – enough even to throw away to the dogs and crows.'

'Bah! . . .' Elias said, sitting silently in a corner. 'Now you've gone too far, papa.'

'Let him talk . . .' Mattia murmured, happy about his father's bragging.

'Shut up, my son. You know nothing about these things. You were born yesterday. But what are you doing, young men? Drink, drink, what the devil! Man is born to drink, and we are men.'

'We are all men,' he concluded philosophically, in a pacifying tone. 'You are men and we are men, and we have to put up with each other. Today you have the swords and represent the king, may the devil stay away from him, but tomorrow? Well, tomorrow it could be that you represent nothing, and it could be that Zio Portolu might then be useful to you. Because

I'm goodhearted – ha, the whole town can tell you that; there are few men like Zio Berte. But my sons also are goodhearted; they have hearts like doves. Well, if you pass by our sheepfold we will give you milk, cheese and even honey. Eh, we also have honey, we do! But you, young men, close an eye, or even both eyes, don't tell the king everything you see, because after all we are men, we are all apt to make mistakes . . .'

The two young men would laugh, drink, and would if necessary really close an eye or even both eyes to the weaknesses of Portolu and their friends.

With regard to friends, even those bad companions came to see Elias – those on whom he and his family blamed the 'misfortune'. In spite of his resolve not to see them, even to close the door in their faces if they dared to come, he welcomed them like a Christian, and Zia Annedda gave them something to drink.

'What can you do?' she said, when they had gone away. 'We have to be Christians, we have to have pity. May God pardon them!'

'And then it's better to keep peace with everyone. The Lord commands peace,' replied Elias.

'Bless you, Elias, you have spoken a great truth.'

Ah, how happy Zia Annedda felt when her son spoke of God! And when she saw him going to mass; and when he read the big black book he had brought from *that place.*

'God be praised!' she thought, greatly moved. 'He's gone back to being as good as he was when a little boy.'

In the meantime mother and son prepared themselves to fulfil their vow to St Francis.

The church of St Francis is in the mountains of Lula. Legend says it was built by a bandit who, tired of his wandering life, promised to give himself up to the law and have the church built if he were acquitted. In any case, true or not, the priors (that is, those who are in charge of the feast) come every year, chosen by the descendants of the founder or founders of the church. All these descendants (who also say they are relatives of St Francis) form a kind of community at the time of the festival and novena, and enjoy certain privileges. The Portolus were among them. A few days before departure Pietro went to St Francis with his cart and oxen, and worked for nothing, along with other farmers and masons – some of them worked because of vows they had made. They put the church and the little rooms built around it into good condition, and brought in wood to be burned during the time of the novena. Zia Annedda, for her part, sent a certain amount of wheat to the prioress, and together with the other women of the tribe of descendants from the church's founders helped clean the flour and make bread to take to the novena. A part of this bread was delivered by the prior's messenger to the sheepfolds around the countryside of Nuoro. To each sheepfold a loaf of bread. The shepherds received it with devotion, and in exchange gave what they could of their produce; some even gave money and live lambs. Others promised to give whole cows that would go towards increasing the herds of the saint, already rich in land, money and flocks.

When the messenger arrived at the Portolu's

sheepfold, Zio Berte took off his hat, made the sign of the cross, kissed the bread. 'I won't give you anything,' he said to the messenger, 'but on the day of the feast I will be there next to my little wife, and I will bring an unsheared sheep to the saint and all my flocks' products of one day. Zio Portolu is not miserly and believes in St Francis, and St Francis has always helped him. Now go with God.'

Zia Annedda in the meanwhile continued her preparations. She made a special bread, biscuits and sweets with almonds and honey; she bought coffee, a sweet liqueur and other provisions. Elias followed affectionately the calm preparations of his mother. Sometimes he helped her. He almost never left the house; he felt exhausted, weak, and often his blue-green eyes, a little hollow, had a glassy stare, and seemed lost in an emptiness, a nothingness. They seemed like the eyes of a dead man.

Departure day finally arrived. It was a Sunday, early in May. Everything was ready in woollen saddlebags; and here and there on the roads were to be seen carts loaded with implements and provisions, with the oxen yoked for the departure.

Zia Annedda and Elias went to hear mass in the little church of Rosario before leaving. Before the mass began a man from the town came in. He went to an altar and took a little shrine made of wood and glass; inside was a statuette of St Francis. As he got ready to leave some women motioned for him to come to them and let them kiss it. Elias also called him with a nod of his head and kissed the glass at the saint's feet.

27

In a short while everyone set off. The prior, a townsman, still young, with an almost blond beard, mounted a beautiful grey horse and carried the standard and the shrine. Other townsmen followed him, with their women sitting behind; there were women riding alone, women on foot, children, carts, dogs. Each one, however, travelling on his own, some ahead, some behind on the road.

Elias, with Zia Annedda sitting behind him on a docile white-footed horse, was among the last; a small colt, son of the horse, little larger than a dog, followed them closely.

It was a beautiful morning. They travelled towards sturdy blue mountains with the sky still lit by dawn's violet flames. The wild valley of Isalle was covered with grass and flowers; along the rocky path bushes of golden yellow broom stood like large burning lanterns. Cool Mount Orthobene, coloured by the green of its woods, by the gold of its broom, by the red flower of moss, retreated behind the travellers, against a pearly background. Suddenly the valley opened up. Solitary flatlands appeared, covered with tender corn shining with dew that had a wavering silvery luminosity under the low sun's rays. The meadows covered with poppies, thyme and daisies gave off piquant odours.

But the wayfarers had to go up into the mountains and so turned away from the flatlands leading to the sea. The sun began to beat strongly, and the rough horsemen from Nuoro began to drink, to 'cool their throats', stopping their horses from time to time and turning their faces up to the carved gourds full of wine.

Everyone was in high spirits. Some spurred on their horses every so often, letting them go at an easy canter, then at an unbridled gallop, leaning backwards, emitting wild yelps of joy.

Elias followed them with his eyes, and his face brightened; he wanted to shout too, he felt a shudder through his loins, an instinctive memory of races long ago, a need to hurl himself again into a quick gallop, into a free and intoxicating race; but Zia Annedda's thin little arm held him around his waist, and he not only restrained his primitive instinct, but remained far enough behind the rest of the riders so that the dust they raised would not bother the little old woman.

Finally they began to climb the mountain. Thick mastic bushes rose and fell among the dull shine of schist, studded with brier roses in full bloom. The horizon stretched out wide and pure, a perfumed wind undulated through the deep green open spaces: ineffable dream of peace, of wild solitude, of an immense silence barely disturbed by the far-off call of a cuckoo and the travellers' muted voices. And then, suddenly, the sublime landscape profaned and desolated by the black gaping mouths dug out by the miners. And then again the peace, dream, splendour of the sky, of dark rocks, of remote seas; again the uninterrupted reign of mastic, of brier roses, of wind, of solitude.

At a certain point, on a level place, high up among the mastic, everyone stopped. Some women dismounted, the men drank. Tradition says that the statue of the saint wanted to stop there while they were carrying it to the little church, and that it wanted a drink! The church could be discerned, with its white walls and red roofs, set halfway down the slope within the green of the bushes.

After a brief rest the journey was taken up again. Elias Portolu and Zia Annedda remained the last. Their goal drew nearer; the sun rose to its zenith, but the pleasant wind, perfumed with brier roses, tempered the intense heat.

They reached the bottom of the little valley, then climbed once again. The white walls, the red roofs were nearer. Be strong, the climb is hard and dry, hang on tight to Elias' waist, Zia Annedda! The horse is tired, glistening all over with sweat; the colt can go no further. Courage. Encampment is near; there it is, the beautiful church with little houses built around it, with the courtyard, the wall, the wide-open gate. It is like a castle all white and red against the intense blue of the sky, on the savage green of the waving grasses.

From below Elias and Zia Annedda saw the horses and riders pushing to form a group so that they could enter the opened gate together, in a cloud of dust. The men lost their caps, the women their kerchiefs; some clung to their flying hair, loosened by the frantic ride. A shrill bell rang from above, and its little strokes of joy were broken and lost in that immensity of blue sky and green country.

Elias and Zia Annedda were the last to enter. In the courtyard invaded by wild grasses, full of burning sun, was a bustling of men and women, a confusion of tired and sweating animals. Children cried, dogs barked.

Flying swallows screeched over the courtyard, almost frightened by seeing that great mountain solitude so suddenly animated. And it really seemed as if a wandering tribe had come a great distance to attack that little uninhabited village. The little doors were opened, the roofs echoed with shouts and laughter.

Elias tranquilly helped his mother dismount, then dismounted himself, tied up his horse and carried on his shoulders, one after the other, the saddlebags stuffed full of their provisions and blankets. And the Portolus, like all the others of the tribe of church founders, took their place in the *cumbissia maggiore*. This *cumbissia* is a very long, dark room, roughly paved, with an under-roof of cane. At intervals are *focolare* of stone in the floor, and large pegs on the rough walls. Each of these pegs indicates the hereditary spot for one of the families descended from the founders.

The Portolus took possession of their peg and their *focolare* at the end of the *cumbissia*, which really was not very lively that year. Only six families lived there, the rest of the pilgrims did not belong to this group, and therefore stayed in the numerous other little rooms.

However, the prior with his family (whose place of honour was distinguished by a wall closet with doors) took up space for two or three families. The prior's family was numerous, with a splendid prioress, fat and white as a cow, two pretty daughters and a brood of little children already dressed in costume. The littlest, still in swaddling clothes, was barely a year old; luckily among the furniture belonging to the church was a little white wooden cradle, where the baby was immediately laid.

The Portolus were quickly settled. Zia Annedda put her basket of sweets, her bread, her coffee in a hole in the wall. On the *focolare* she put her coffee pot and pan; along the wall she laid her sack, blanket, red pillow, and put out the cane basket with the cups and plates. That was everything. For neighbours the Portolus had a little bent-over widow with two grandchildren; they quickly made friends, exchanging presents and compliments. After this Elias unsaddled his horse and let it and the colt graze freely in the grass nearby.

While the shouting, the coming and going, the confusion continued in the courtyard and little rooms, Zia Annedda went to the church to pray: a cool, clean little church, with marble flooring, and a large, bearded saint, in truth more inspiring of fear than affection. Soon afterwards Elias also went into the church; he knelt on the altar steps, with his cap on his shoulder, and prayed.

Zia Annedda gazed at him intently, praying fervently. It seemed as though he were the saint to whom her motherly prayers were directed. Ah, that tired, delicate profile, that white sickly face, what tenderness it awoke in her! To see him there, her beloved son kneeling at the feet of the saint, fulfilling the vow made in faraway lands, in disagreeable places – ah, that was a thing that melted Zia Annedda's heart.

'Ah, *Santu Franziscu bellu*, my little St Francis, I don't have the words to thank you. Take my life if you like, everything you want, but let my sons be happy, let them go on the Lord's straight and narrow path, let them not be too attached to the things of this world, my *Santu Franzischeddu*!'

Little by little the coming and going, the hubbub, the confusion stopped. Each one had taken his place, even the very illustrious chaplain, a priest, just a little over four feet tall, very red in the face, very happy, who whistled the latest tunes and hummed café-concert melodies.

The horses were put to pasture; fires were lit in the *focolare*; and the splendid prioress and the women of the group began to cook large cauldrons of soup flavoured with fresh cheese. What a gay life then began for this peaceful and patriarchal clan! Sheep and lambs were butchered, heaps of macaroni cooked, much coffee, wine, *aquavite* drunk. The chaplain said the mass and novena, whistled and hummed.

However, the greatest amusement was had in the large *cumbissia* at night around the high crackling fires of mastic. Outside the night was cool, sometimes almost cold. The moon rose on the vast west, giving a wild enchantment to the scrubland. O pale nights of Sardinian solitude! The pulsing owl's cry, the wild fragrance of thyme, the sharp odour of the mastic trees, the distant murmur of solitary woods made a monotonous melancholic harmony that gave a feeling of solemn sadness, a nostalgia for things ancient and pure.

Gathering around the fire, the citizens of the large *cumbissia* told witty stories, drank and sang. The echo

33

of their sonorous voices was lost in the beyond, in that great solitude, in that lunar silence, among the scrub where the horses slept.

Elias Portolu took part in the entertainment with intense, almost childish pleasure. He seemed to be in a new world. He told about his vicissitudes and eagerly listened to the stories of the others.

Besides, he had formed a close relationship with the chaplain, and this new friend spoke to him in an amusing way, urging him to enjoy life, to forget, to have a good time.

'Serve God in gladness,' he told him. 'Let's dance, sing, whistle, enjoy ourselves. God has given us life to enjoy it a little. I don't say to sin, huh! Ah, not that! And then sin leaves remorse, a torment, my dear boy . . . enough, you've probably tried it. But honest enjoyment, yes, yes, yes! My name is Jacu Maria Porcu, or Father Porcheddu because I am small. Jacu Maria Porcu has enjoyed himself much in his lifetime. Well done! One night I came home after midnight. My sister says I was drunk; but I don't think so, dear boy. "What did you fix for my supper, Anna?" "I'll give you nothing, nothing, Jacu Maria Porcu, for shame; it's past midnight. I'm giving you nothing." "Give me something to eat, Annesa; you have to give a priest something to eat." "Oh, well, I'll give you bread and cheese, for shame, Jacu Maria Porcu, for shame, it's past midnight." "Bread and cheese to a priest, to Jacu Maria Procu?" "Yes, bread and cheese. Here it is if you want it, if not just leave it." "Bread and cheese to Jacu Maria Porcu? To Father

34

Porcheddu? Here doggie, doggie, take it," and Father Porcheddu threw it all to the dogs! And so one must do, young man with the pale face! And just because I'm a priest I mustn't enjoy myself? Enjoy, yes; sin, no!

> 'We make love for fun,
> We make love for fun,
> For nothing more than fun,
> You today, tomorrow another!'

'He's crazy!' thought Elias, laughing, but he was amused, and Father Porcheddu's words impressed him, brought him a breath of life, a desire to sing, enjoy himself, have a good time.

Almost every day he, Father Porcheddu, the prior and some other friends went far off, into the shade of the tall bushes. Everyone was silent in the metallic quiet of the afternoon; before them the picturesque mountains of Lula stood out clear and blue against the pure sky, and in the distance, on the green of the scrubland, the horses frolicked, chasing each other in circles. And the friends, comfortably stretched out on the grass, one after the other, recounted their more or less adventurous pasts, the legends of the church, jokes about women, epics of the ancient Sardinians. Often the conversation was interrupted by a warbling, by a little whistle from Father Porcheddu. Sometimes the chaplain would even jump up suddenly to his feet, doing little kicking steps, or he would sing, accompanying his popular song with absurd gestures.

One day, the day before the eve of the feast, they were like this in the shade of a cluster of large mastic trees. Elias had finished telling how once a fellow prisoner had beaten a prison warden because he had discourteously refused an invitation to drink with some of the prisoners, when a trembling, sharp whistle was heard, coming like an arrow from the direction of the church.

Elias jumped up on his feet, shouting, 'That's my brother Pietro's whistle.'

'Well,' said Father Porcheddu, 'if it's your brother, you'll be glad to see each other! Why are you so anxious?'

'My father must have come, too, and maybe even Pietro's fiancée. Let's go, let's go . . .' Elias said, very agitated.

'If it's like that, let's go,' said the prior. 'We must show them respect. Berte Portolu is a good patron of St Francis. And then Maria Maddalena Scada is a pretty girl.'

'A pretty girl?' exclaimed Father Porcheddu. 'If it's like that, let's go!'

Elias looked at him scornfully; but Father Porcheddu faced that look and then laughed, singing his favourite song:

> 'We make love for fun,
> For nothing more than fun,
> For nothing more than fun . . .'

And then they set off for the church on a barely visible path through scrub and bushes and fragrant green grass. The whistle was repeated, ever closer and more insistent. Elias was not mistaken. Pietro and Zio

Portolu were standing in front of the well; between them was the luminous shape of Maria Maddalena. Elias felt a blow to his heart. Father Porcheddu clicked his tongue against his palate and was silent, finding no words for his admiration. And he claimed to have had experience with women!

Maddalena was not very tall, nor truly beautiful, but most attractive, slender, with a very fair rosy-brown complexion, shining eyes under thick brows, and a sensual mouth. Her scarlet-red corset opened over a white blouse, and her flowered kerchief of orchids and roses made her dazzling. Between the rough figures of Pietro and Zio Portolu, she seemed like grace amid savage strength. Up close her slightly slanted, shining eyes, half-closed and a bit voluptuous, with long lashes, were fascinating in the true sense of the word.

'Welcome,' said Elias coming closer and shaking her hand. 'Have you been here long? You weren't expected until tomorrow.'

'Tomorrow or today is the same thing,' Zio Portolu replied. 'Greetings to all of you, to the prior, to that little red priest. God defend him. You can tell he's a priest, even if he's wearing trousers.'

'Father Porcheddu, what do you say to that?'

'With trousers or without, we are all men,' he responded, a little piqued. Then he turned to Maddalena and began paying her compliments.

'Watch out,' Elias said smiling, 'Father Porcheddu is terrible with the women.'

'No more than you are,' replied the little priest quickly.

Maddalena laughed sweetly. 'I'm not afraid of anyone.'

And Zio Portolu: 'Don't be afraid of anyone, my girl, my dove, fear no one. Zio Portolu is here, and if Zio Portolu isn't enough, there's also his *leppa*.'

He removed the large knife he carried in his belt from its sheath, brandishing it in the air. Father Porcheddu backed off, holding out his hands in a pretended comic gesture of terror.

'This is Mohammed! This is a scimitar! Watch out!'

'What do you want?' said Zio Portolu, putting his *leppa* back in place. 'This girl, this dove, has been entrusted to me by her mother, a widowed dove. "Arrita Scada," I said to her, "don't worry, the dove will be safe in my hands. I will defend her even against my son, golden Pietro, as well as against the other hawks and vultures."'

Zio Portolu was speaking seriously; and every once in a while he turned wild looks of affection on the girl.

'When it's like that we pay attention,' observed Father Porcheddu. 'And now let's drink.'

'Drink, yes, bravo Father Porcheddu! One who doesn't drink isn't a man, nor even a priest.'

They began walking. Zia Annedda was waiting for them with her coffee pot and her decanters and her large baskets of sweets. Maddalena and her retinue erupted into the *cumbissia* laughing and chattering; in short, it was a chaos of voices, shouts, laughter, a tinkling of glasses and cups. Zio Portolu could be heard telling how he had made the whole trip with the

38

sheep promised to St Francis tied over his horse's flank.

'It was my best sheep!' he said to the prior. 'Such long wool. Eh, Zio Portolu is not a miser.'

'Go to the devil!' the prior responded. 'Don't you see it's as old and whiteheaded as you are!'

'You're whiteheaded, Antoni Carta! If you insult me again I'll put my *leppa* in you.'

Father Porcheddu held his glass high, his head inclined a little towards his shoulder, his flattering eyes turned toward Maddalena and the prior's pretty daughters.

> 'On the stern of my brig,
> Smoking good cigars,
> With the glass going clink,
> I drink smugglers' rum.'

'Ha! Ha! Ha!' the women laughed.

Only Elias was silent. Sitting on one of the many saddles scattered around the *cumbissia*, he sipped his wine, raising and lowering his head from time to time. And every time he raised his eyes he met the smiling eyes of Maddalena, sitting opposite him a short distance away, and those slanting burning eyes penetrated his soul. He felt a kind of intoxication, a relaxing of all his nerves, an almost physical pleasure every time he looked at her.

The voices, chatter, laughter, Father Porcheddu's songs, the women's exclamations, came to him as from a distance. He seemed to be listening from a remote place, without taking part. But suddenly someone

39

began talking to him, bringing him back to himself; he woke up as from a dream, his face darkened, he got up and went out swiftly.

'Where are you going, Elias!' shouted Pietro, joining him.

'I'm going to look at the horses. Let me go!' he answered almost rudely.

'The horses are settled. Why are you in such a bad mood, Elias? Are you sorry that Maddalena came?'

'Of course not! Why do you say that?' asked Elias, looking at him.

'No, it seems like you're sulking. It seems you don't like her. What do you say, my brother?'

'You're crazy! You are all crazy! Even she, with all her exalted sensibleness, laughs too much.'

Pietro was not offended. Besides, he and everyone at home treated Elias like a child, or rather like a sick man. They were afraid to cause him displeasure, and so tried to make him happy in every way. Even at this time, seeing that he wanted to be left alone, Pietro went back to his fiancée.

'They're all crazy,' Elias thought as he wandered here and there. 'And me too? Ah, she'll be the wife of my brother. Why am I so crazy as to look at her?'

He stayed outside all evening.

'Where in the world is Elias?' Zia Annedda asked every once in a while, looking around restlessly. 'Where could that blessed young man have gone? Go and look for him, Pietro.'

But Pietro's eyes were following Maddalena – who to tell the truth didn't seem very much in love with him, or at least she didn't show it, perhaps to keep her composure following her mother's advice – and he would answer: 'I'm going, I'm going,' but he didn't move.

'Where can Elias be?' Zia Annedda repeated when the supper hour arrived. 'Portolu, go and find your son.'

Zio Berte, sitting on the ground next to the *focolare*, was roasting a whole lamb skewered on a wooden spit. He was bragging that no one in the world could roast a lamb or a pig better than he.

'I'll go, I'll go,' he answered his wife, 'let me settle accounts with this little beast first.'

'The lamb is roasted, Berte; go and look for your son.'

'The lamb is not roasted, my little wife. What do you know about it? Oh, what's wrong with you that you advise Berte Portolu about this? Let the boys have fun, anyway; they need to enjoy themselves.'

But she insisted, and Zio Berte was getting ready to go when Elias came back in. His eyes were shining, his face burning: he was beautiful. Everyone looked at him, and Zia Annedda sighed, and Zio Berte began laughing with pleasure, realizing that Elias was a little drunk.

But Elias saw only the slanting, burning eyes of Maddalena, and felt like crying like a baby.

'She's crazy!' he thought. 'Why does she look at me like that? Why doesn't she leave me in peace? I'm going to tell Pietro, I'll tell everyone. And if she doesn't love him, why does she deceive him? She's

41

crazy, crazy, but so am I. I don't have to look at her. I have to get her off my mind. Now I'll go over there to Paska, the prior's daughter, and court her . . .'

'Paska,' he said out loud, going near the prior's *focolare*, 'you are the most beautiful relative of St Francis.'

'And you're the handsomest,' the girl responded readily, bustling around a steaming pot.

Elias sat down next to her, looking at her with a strange intensity. She laughed happily, but within his heart he felt himself dying.

At the back of the *cumbissia* Maddalena was watching him, and every once in a while she lowered her wide eyes, seeming then like a melancholy, resigned madonna. When supper was ready Zio Berte called Elias.

'I'm staying here,' shouted the young man, 'the prettiest relative of St Francis has invited me to her *focolare*'.

'You come here!' shouted Zio Portolu. 'No one has invited you, but even if they had invited you, I wouldn't allow it . . . If you won't come properly, Zio Portolu, your father, will force you.'

Elias rose immediately and obeyed. But he didn't want to eat or drink, and made little response if someone tried to talk to him.

'Why are you in such bad humour?' Maddalena asked him nicely, while they finished eating. 'Because we took you away from the prior's *focolare*? Go on back, be happy.'

'And if I went back?' he responded roughly, 'what would that matter to you?'

'Ah, nothing!' she said stiffening. Then she turned to Pietro and, smiling, paid attention only to him.

Elias jumped to his feet and went away; but instead of stopping again at the prior's *focolare* he went outside and sat in the courtyard. He felt a confused, feverish anxiety, a desire to bite his fists, to shout, to throw himself on the ground and cry. And yet, in the intoxication of wine and passion, he still preserved a self-awareness, and thought: 'I'm in love with her; why am I in love, my St Francis? Help me, help me! I'm crazy, my St Francis, but I'm so unhappy!'

From the *cumbissias* the mixture of voices, songs and laughter floated outside, vibrant in the silence of the warm, pure night. Elias distinguished his father's voice, Father Porcheddu's whistle, Maddelena's laugh, and amid such festivities he felt sad, desperate, like a child left alone in the wild nocturnal solitude of the scrubland.

III

Gradually the noise died down and silence fell over that sleeping clan. Elias went back inside and lay down beside Pietro, on the same bundle of pungent grass. Grass pallets were scattered all over the *cumbissia*; some fires were still burning, sending a quavering rosy gleam over that vast silent scene. Here a long beard could be seen, there a woollen costume, a woman's face, a saddle, a dog huddled next to the *focolare*, a rifle hanging on the wall. Elias couldn't sleep; he seemed to be breathing in Maddalena's breath as she lay between Zia Annedda and Zio Portolu, and he continued to feel a desperate desire for her; but he struggled against it.

'No, don't be afraid, my brother,' he said to himself, turning toward Pietro, 'even if she threw herself at me, I would push her away. I don't want her, she's yours. If she belonged to someone else I would take her away

44

from him, even at the cost of returning to one of *those places*; but she's yours. Sleep in peace, my brother. I'll take a wife, too, soon, right away. I'll ask Paska, the prior's daughter.'

'Oh, well,' he then thought, 'I'm an idiot. Why do I need a wife, why should I think about women? I can live without women. Oh, didn't I live three years without even laying eyes on one? Could that be the reason why, just when I get back home, I fall in love with the first woman I see? But I'm crazy. Forget about women who make you crazy. Just go to sleep.'

But he tossed and turned, and couldn't sleep. And so it went nearly the whole night, and he was also among the first to wake up. From the open window framing a silvery background came the dewy coolness of dawn; Zia Annedda and Maddalena, still sleepy, were already making coffee. Elias got up, pale as a cadaver, with his hair rumpled and his throat swollen.

'Good morning,' Maddalena said, smiling at him. 'Look, Zia Annedda, your son's face is the colour of wax. Quick, quick, give him some coffee.'

'Aren't you feeling well, my son?'

'I think I've caught cold,' he said hoarsely, clearing his throat. 'Give me something to drink. Where is your pitcher?'

He looked around, took the pitcher, and drank deeply. Maddalena watched him and laughed.

'Why are you laughing?' he said, putting the pitcher down. 'Because I drink as soon as I get up? That means that last night I was drunk. All right then, wine was made for men.'

45

'You aren't a man,' Zio Portolu broke in, who had already drunk some *aquavite*. 'You're a puppet made of fresh cheese; a woman just has to blow on you, puff . . . for you to fall down dead, done for.'

'All right, so be it,' said Elias, irritated. 'I'll drop dead if some woman just blows on me, but everyone just leave me alone.'

'Ah, what a bad mood you're in!' exclaimed Maddalena. 'Is it because I'm here?'

'Yes, exactly, because you're here.'

'The dove!' Zio Portolu shouted, taking her by the arm. 'The dove that gladdens wherever she goes. And my son, this puppet with a cat's eyes, says that you put him in a bad mood? Go, go, go, do me a favour, go away, son of the devil! If you're in a bad mood go and hang yourself; but you'll certainly never bring another rose like this one to Zio Portolu, to cheer up his house.'

These words struck Elias to the heart, because suddenly he remembered that Maddalena would have to live in their house as Pietro's bride in a few weeks. Ah, what torture it would be! No, he couldn't stand it.

'Drink this coffee, my son,' said Zia Annedda. 'Take this cake, be happy because we are at the feast, and St Francis will be offended if we're sad.'

'But I am happy, mamma, I'm happy as a bird. Hey!' he then shouted, turning toward the prior's *focolare*, 'Good morning, pretty Paska.'

After that nothing interesting happened that day or the next at the Portolus' *focolare*. On the eve of the feast

46

many people arrived from Nuoro and nearby towns; from Lula particularly, over the steep mountain path through the glowing broom bushes, long lines of women descended dressed in costumes a bit overdone, with their heads exaggeratedly elongated by caps under large fringed kerchiefs, with very short, heavy skirts of coarse woollen fabric, and long rosaries fastened by elaborate silver ornaments.

The Portolus also had many guests, and Elias and Pietro were dragged here and there all day by the young men who had come from Nuoro for the feast. They all drank until they lost their reason, sang, danced, yelled. At times Elias seemed crazy; he laughed until he turned purple, with his green eyes, and let out strange shouts of joy, ayyee - long, guttural, vibrating - that seemed to be calling wild warriors to battle.

Maddalena, who helped Zia Annedda prepare the meals, serve the wine and coffee to the guests, looked sideways at him every once in a while and murmured: 'Your son is very happy, Zia Anna; look how red-faced he is. How he laughs!'

Zia Annedda looked at Elias, sighed, and felt a thorn in her heart; and when she had a free moment she went in the church and prayed.

'Ah, *Santu Franziscu meu*, beautiful, wonderful St Francis, take this thorn from my heart. Elias, my son, is going back to bad ways. There he is, drunk, excited, no longer the one he was. He seemed so good after he came back, and promised so many things! Have pity on us, St Francis, my little St Francis, put him on the

47

right path again, convert him, keep him from vice, from bad companions, from the things of this world. St Francis, my little brother, grant me this grace!'

The great severe, almost grim saint listened from the high altar that had been enthusiastically embellished with every kind of flowering plant. It seemed he had answered Zia Annedda's prayer, because that same evening at supper Elias revealed his plan. They were talking about Father Porcheddu: some criticized him, others laughed at him.

Elias, still drunk, that is true, but only slightly, defended his friend, then he said: 'Oh, well, bark away, mangy dogs, run him down. He doesn't give a damn. He's better than the pope. And I'm going to be a priest, too.'

Everyone laughed.

He said: 'Why are you laughing, you begging devils, mangy dogs, you animals? I know how to read Latin. And I hope to bring all of you the Last Sacraments and bury you beggars.'

'Even me, brother dear?' shouted Pietro.

'Yes, even you.'

And Maddalena: 'Even me?'

'Even you!' shouted Elias, fiercely. 'And why not you? Because you're a woman? Men and women are the same to me, or rather, women are more vile than men.'

'All this doesn't matter,' said Zio Portolu, who was listening carefully to Elias' words. 'Let's get back to the subject. You would like to become a priest, then?'

'That's what it looks like!' shouted Elias pouring a

drink. 'Drink, drink, pour it out, swill it down.'

They filled their glasses to the top.

'Easy, easy,' yelled Zio Portolu in the general gaiety. 'Let's reason a little before drinking . . .'

'If you don't drink you aren't a man, papa dear,' said Pietro, repeating the axiom his father so often said. But the latter was really angry, and said more quietly, 'Even beasts reason, son of the devil! Respect your father, and be thankful for the presence of these friends and this dove, otherwise I'd give you as many slaps as you have hairs on your head.'

'Bah! Bah! Zio Portolu! This is too much! To talk to a groom like that!'

'Maddalena mine, I'm lost if you don't help me,' shouted Pietro, laughing.

'Dove, help him!' said Zio Portolu sarcastically; then he turned again to Elias and asked him if he was really serious. But Elias was drinking, laughing, shouting, and didn't answer, and the announcement of his bizarre plan had already vanished in the noisy hilarity of the guests.

But someone had heard him with anxiety: Zia Annedda. She kept silent, partly out of modesty, and partly because she had not been able to understand clearly what they were saying, but she looked around searchingly. Maddalena whispered in her ear every now and then, repeating this and that. Zia Annedda would nod her head and smile. Ah, if Elias had been talking seriously! But was it possible? Such a great miracle! Ah, but St Francis could perform that miracle and others. Elias was still young, he could

49

study, he could succeed. And that was His way, the Lord's Way, because if Elias remained in the world he was lost. Zia Annedda was thinking along these lines because she knew her son.

The first moment she had free she went into the church to thank the saint for the idea sent to Elias. It was night; the lantern wavered in front of the altar, spreading quivering shadows and light throughout the deserted church. The great gloomy saint seemed drowsy among his many flowers. Zia Annedda genuflected, then sat at the back of the church, praying. Her thoughts always turned to Elias. It seemed she could already see her priest son; she seemed already to be receiving the gifts of wheat, the little bottles of wine stoppered with flowers, the cakes and the *gattos*.

While dreaming and praying like this she saw Maddalena enter. The young woman had come looking for her; she sat down next to Zia Annedda.

'Ah, here you are!' she said. 'We've been looking for you, but suddenly I thought you would be here.'

'I'll come in a little while.'

'I'll stay here a little while, too.'

They were silent. From the courtyard came a mixture of sounds, songs and melancholy tunes, vibrating in the pure night. A harmonious tenor was singing Nuorese songs to a sad, rhythmical choral accompaniment. And those nostalgic songs and sounds that seemed impregnated with the solemn sadness of the brushwood, the night, the solitude, rose, spread over the sounds of the crowd, filling the air with flowering dreams.

Maddalena listened, gripped by a profound sadness. Now and again she seemed to recognize that voice. Was it Pietro? Was it Elias? She didn't know, she didn't know, but that voice and that chorus softly fading in the night gave her an almost morbid, sad pleasure. And Zia Annedda continued dreaming, praying, without realizing that Maddalena trembled and shook next to her as though she really were a smitten dove.

But then suddenly the thoughts of the two women were stopped in their course; a figure entered and walked uncertainly toward the altar. It was the man who occupied both their minds: Elias. Elias kneeled on the altar steps with his cap over his right shoulder and began to beat his breast, his head, and to groan quietly. The flickering reddish lamplight illuminated him from above, reflected on his hair; but he did not think anyone could see him and so continued in his sorrowful fervour to moan and beat his breast and forehead.

The two women looked at him, holding their breath, and Zia Annedda felt almost happy about her son's sorrow. 'He regrets being drunk,' she thought, 'he has good intentions: bless you, my St Francis, my little St Francis.'

'Come, let's leave before he sees us and is ashamed,' she said under her breath to Maddalena, pulling her out of the church.

'What's wrong with Elias?' asked Maddalena, disturbed.

'He's sorry about drinking so much; he's very devout, my daughter.'

'Oh!'

'Sometimes he is impulsive, but he is a conscientious young man, my daughter. Ah, very conscientious.'

'Oh!'

'Yes, very conscientious, my daughter. He can be led into temptation, because you know that the devil is always doing his work around us, but Elias knows how to fight him and would die before committing a mortal sin. At times temptation overcomes him in little things, like today; you saw how he got drunk and talked roughly; but then he bitterly regrets it.'

'Oh!' Maddalena said for the third time; and she didn't know why, but she felt her eyes burning with tears.

They crossed the courtyard and re-entered the *cumbissia* where Zio Portolu, Pietro and their friends were sitting around the *focolare* singing and playing cards. Maddalena sat down in the shadow, to the side of the small window, more serious and quiet than usual; Pietro went to her and looked at her intently.

'You're so serious, Maddalena. Why? Have you seen Elias? Did he say something to you?'

'No, I haven't seen him.'

'Elias is in a bad mood. Let him talk, you know, don't pay any attention to him; he treats everyone like that.'

'But it doesn't matter!' she exclaimed brightly. 'And anyway he didn't say anything discourteous to me.'

52

'But then you are discreet. Isn't it true that you're discreet?' said Pietro coaxingly, passing a hand across her shoulders.

'Leave me alone!' she said sharply. 'Go and play cards.'

'No, I'm staying here, Maddalena.'

'Go!'

'No!'

'Zio Portolu, tell your son to go back to his game.'

'Pietro, my son, leave the dove in peace. Come here at once! Or do you want me to make you obey with my walking stick?'

Pietro took his place.

'Eh, eh, the old fox makes them obey!' someone said.

Maddalena turned towards the window and looked outside, with her mind far from the noisy scene she had turned her back on, her beautiful eyes lost in a sad dream. It was a warm, overcast night; the moon sailed towards the south, in a lake of silvery vapours. The black bushes in the scrubland fading into the grey background smelled sweeter than usual.

Maddalena was thinking of Elias; and here, for the second time, almost evoked by her unconscious suggestion, the figure of Elias rose before her. He passed under the window; he went away in that vaporous moonlight. Where was he going? Where was he going? Maddalena felt tears well up in her eyes, and a shudder ran through her body and swelled up in her throat.

She would have liked to jump out of the window, to

run after Elias, to envelop him and smother him with her passion. But he disappeared in the distance, and she secretly swallowed her tears.

Elias had made his vow, he had said mentally to his brother: 'Sleep in peace, Pietro, my brother; she is young, and even if she threw herself at me I would push her away.'

The wine vapours having vanished, he felt strong, and after the crisis that had dragged him to the feet of the saint, almost happy. All the desperate plans, fomented by the liquor and by Maddalena's glances, that had spun in his brain that day – the idea of becoming a priest, of asking for the hand of the prior's daughter – all had evaporated with the drunkenness. Now he felt not only calm but also a little ashamed of what he had thought and said during that disturbing day.

He went to look at the horses that were grazing tranquilly under the moon, he gave them water and then turned towards the church.

'Tomorrow I'll go back,' he thought. 'The day after that to the sheepfold. I'll stay away from town for months, with my father and that simpleton Mattia, with my shepherd friends. What a pleasant life! After I've been alone there for a long time, these days, all this foolishness will seem like a dream. Eh, feasts are nice and the saints are good, but the wine, the people, the enjoyment set the blood afire, and if you aren't very very wise, you can fall into great error and be led into temptation. Ah, well, now I'll go to bed and sleep because I didn't sleep a wink last night; then tomorrow

... away ... and the day after I'll go far, far away. Eh, Elias Portolu, are you afraid of yourself? ... But what do I see there? A man sleeping under that bush; no, it's not a man; well what is it then? Yes, it's a man ... oh, Father Porcheddu! ...'

Surprised, he bent over and shook the sleeping man.

'Hey, hey, Father Porcheddu! What's this? Why are you here? Don't you know that this air could be bad for you, that there are snakes and insects in the grass?'

After many vigorous shakes Father Porcheddu woke up in a daze. He tried to recognize Elias, opening his eyes wide many times, and finally came to himself and got up.

'Eh, well, I came out after supper, I wanted to take a walk, but it seems I went to sleep.'

'It seems like that to me, too! If I hadn't seen you by chance, you would have stayed here until who knows when, and who knows how frightened we would have been if you hadn't come back!'

'Don't think that I drank too much, dear boy, no. I came out like I said, and seeing the moon, I sat down here. Eh, you don't know that I was a poet once?'

'Oh! Oh!'

'Shall we sit here a little? Look at the beautiful night. Yes, I was a poet, and I have published poetry, but as they were love poems, what did the monsignor make me do? He sent word for me to stop, that these were not things for a priest to do.'

'And you, Father Porcheddu? ...'

'I stopped. My son, I know that you have decided I'm crazy . . .'

'Father Porcheddu!'

' . . . a crazy man, but one that doesn't hurt anyone, much less himself. I've always known how to live. I have been happy, but discreet. And so, that time, I stopped, but I haven't lost the habit of daydreaming sometimes. Look – what a beautiful night, my son. It's one of those nights that invite you to think, to examine your life, to be sorry for the wrong done and to make good resolutions for the future. You are intelligent, Elias Portolu, you aren't just any kind of shepherd, you have studied and suffered, and you can understand these things.'

'It's true,' Elias said in a deep voice.

Father Porcheddu, looking up, was watching the moon. Elias also raised his eyes and looked up there. He felt strangely moved.

'That's it, my son,' the other went on, 'you understand all these things. I know that you are intelligent, and you look at the moon not to guess the time, like all the other shepherds, but with high, solemn feeling.' (Nevertheless, Elias didn't understand these last words very well.) 'Perhaps you, too, are a bit of a poet, and you could write love poetry . . .'

'Not that, Father Porcheddu.'

Father Porcheddu was silent for a moment, thoughtful, serious. Then he murmured a verse in dialect. It was an 'Invocation to the month of May'.

56

'May, May, welcome,
With everything of sun and love,
With the palm and flower
And with the marguerite.'

And Elias didn't stop looking at the moon, asking himself if it would be good to compose a poem for . . . Maddalena. Ah, for a moment he had forgotten and the devil had recaptured his dominion! But the voice of Father Porcheddu sounded again, a little serious, a little quavering, subdued and yet energetic in that great silence with the veiled moon, in the deserted, perfumed scrub.

'You're looking at the moon, Elias Portolu, you're thinking of writing a poem . . . Here's what I guess. You're in love.'

'Father Porcheddu! . . .' said Elias, frightened, bowing his head.

He suddenly felt that that man next to him was in possession of his painful secret, and he reddened with shame and anger. He would have liked to throw himself on Father Porcheddu and strangle him.

'You're in love with Maddalena. Eh, don't blush, don't get angry, my son. I guessed it, but don't be afraid, don't think that everyone understands things like Father Porcheddu understands them. And anyway, what's there to be ashamed of? She's a woman, and you're a man, and being a man you have human passions, temptations, your mother Zia Annedda would say. The shame isn't in that, my son; it's in not knowing how to conquer yourself. But you will conquer yourself. Maddalena . . .'

'Talk softly . . .' Elias said.

'Maddalena is a holy thing for you. Looking at her is like looking at a saint. Do you understand? Isn't it true?'

'I . . . I understand . . .' murmured Elias.

'Very well, you understand: I said you were intelligent! Look, why did God create day and night? The day to make it easy for the devil to fight us; the night so we can collect our thoughts and conquer temptation. Nights like this are made for that, because especially in these nights so calm, in the silence, we must remember that our life is short, that death comes when we least expect it, and that from all our life we can only bring our good works, duties fulfilled, temptations overcome before the Lord.'

'And poetry, then?' asked Elias, smiling slightly. And he seemed happy to catch Father Porcheddu in a contradiction, but his voice was troubled.

'Beautiful poetry is the voice of our conscience when it tells us we have done our duty. Eh, what do you say about that, Elias Portolu?'

'I say that's true.'

'Very good. Now we must go. It's beginning to get damp, and then you told me there are snakes. Eh, eh, give me your hand, help me get up . . . Eh I'm not twenty years old, I can't jump up like you. Good, thanks; now let me hold on to you. What do you say about Father Porcheddu?' he then asked, taking Elias' arm. 'He's crazy, he can go to bed late, drink, sing, throw bread to the dogs, but he isn't bad. Your conscience, above all your conscience, Elias Portolu, remember your conscience! Ah, what do I see there? A black thing, look, could it be a snake?'

'No, it's a twig.'

'When they see us coming back like this they'll think I'm drunk. But I don't care because I'm not. Do you think I am?'

'Oh, no!' Elias said emphatically.

'Good, then you'll always remember what I told you!'

'I'll remember.'

'I love your family,' began Father Porcheddu, but immediately regretting these words, he cleverly changed the subject and for the whole hour he stayed with Elias he didn't touch on that sensitive topic.

The name of Maddalena was not mentioned again. But now Elias felt like another person – strong, calm, almost cold, determined to struggle fiercely against himself. Tomorrow morning, the departure. The old prior had turned over the standard, the shrine and the key to the new prior, drawn by lot on the previous day; the prioress had divided the bread and the leftover provisions and the last cauldron of *filindeu* among the families of the large *cumbissia*. At dawn they began preparations for leaving. The carts were loaded, the horses saddled, the saddlebags filled. They left after mass, and the new prior closed the door. The little rooms, the church, the scrub were deserted again, subsiding into the blue background of the solitary mountains.

Addio. The horned owl takes up his prolonged, rhythmical cry, vibrating in the infinite silence of the

59

scrubland. On the nights fragrant with the mastic tree, on the long luminous days, it is the king of solitude, the only ruler, and its melancholy cry seems like the dreamy voice of the landscape. *Addio.* The horses trot, gallop, go up and down through the green hollows of the mountain; the good and proud tribe of the clan and the devotees of St Francis returns to its little town, down there behind the cool slopes of Orthobene, returns to its work, to its sheepfolds, to its crops, to its hard life. The feast is over.

Zio Portolu rode with Zia Annedda on the back of his horse and Pietro brought his fiancée. This time Elias trotted along with those leading the caravan; he also often broke into a gallop, nostrils trembling and eyes burning as though drunk with the warm, perfumed wind that shook the flowering scrub and brushed his face with strong caresses. Deep within, however, he was serious: he didn't sing or shout like the others, and didn't even turn to look at Paska, the daughter of the ex-prior whom he often found himself beside. Paska took every opportunity to give him tender, though timid, glances, but he was thinking: 'Why should I deceive anyone, much less an innocent girl? No, I must not deceive anyone, and much less myself.'

He was remembering Father Porcheddu's words, and the good resolutions he had made the night before: therefore he paid no attention to Paska, stayed away from Maddalena, and without realizing it, tried to escape himself by innocently inebriating himself in galloping and racing his swift horse.

Zio Portolu and Zia Annedda were riding a horse followed by a colt. Pietro and Maddalena had a very docile, lean, frail horse, and so they brought up the rear, and Zio Portolu never ceased watching after them. Towards midday they reached Isalle; following the custom they dismounted there to eat under a group of trees, among rocks covered with flowering moss on the river bank. Encampment was quickly made; fires rose up, spits turned, tables were set. The noontime was mild; big, high oleander bushes rose along the running water, motionless in the warm air; at the end of the valley the wheat gleamed in the sun. The shrine with the little St Francis was placed on a large handkerchief spread out upon the ground, and after the meal men and women crowded around it, kneeling, kissing it and placing an offering inside it. Pietro came with Maddalena, and more for her to see than out of devotion, he put a large offering inside the shrine; then Zia Annedda came, then Elias, who stayed awhile, turning his prayerful eyes to the little saint. Ah, he felt lost again; the heat, the torpor of that serene midday, the wine, the presence of Maddalena tormented him bitterly. But the little saint listened to his prayer and gave him the courage to go away and lie beside the river bank under the oleanders, alone and fortified against temptation.

In the camp the women were chattering, drinking coffee and getting ready to leave. The men sang or did target practice. Elias heard the shots thunder out, run through the valley, repeat themselves in the distant green and bounce back with the echo. He heard voices

61

far away, softened by the quiet noontime; the warbling of finches, the murmuring of running water; and his senses were relaxing into the first sweetness of sleep, when a vision appeared.

It was Maddalena coming down to wash herself. She wasn't upset at seeing him, in fact she bent over him . . . Ah, too much! Too much! Her eyes – burning, fatal – enchanted him. He remembered his vow: 'Pietro, my brother, even if she throws herself at me I'll push her away . . .' But he felt a breathlessness, a delirium that suffocated and blinded him. He would have liked to escape but he couldn't move, and she stood close to him, and her half-closed eyes, burning under the wide lids, and her lips and teeth were making him lose consciousness.

'Maddalena, *amore mio* . . .' he murmured, but immediately repented and began to groan with passion and sorrow. 'Pietro, my brother! Pietro, my brother . . .'

He woke up trembling. He was alone, and the water was murmuring and the birds warbling, but he heard nothing any more, neither shots nor voices. He got up. How long had he slept? He looked at the sun and it was going down. Everyone had gone except the two shepherds who were guarding Elias' horse; the caravan had given them the banquet leftovers in exchange for some milk products. Elias thanked them and left. His horse flew, and the motion and the thought of soon rejoining his companions dispersed the feverish and anxious impression that the dream had left. After almost an hour of riding he saw Zio

62

Portolu and Zia Annedda, Pietro and Maddalena, sitting on their horses at the top of a slope. They were waiting for him perhaps? The others were already far away.

'What's going on?' he shouted from below.

'What the devil got into you?' shouted Zio Portolu, 'what kept you? Give your horse to your brother, because his is worn out.'

'No, I won't give it to him.'

'Elias, my son, obey your father,' said Zia Annedda.

'No,' replied Elias, annoyed. 'You left me behind like a donkey; I'm not giving it to him.'

'All right then. You take Maddalena for a bit. We can't go far like this,' Pietro said.

'Ah, Pietro, what are you saying?' Elias shouted within himself; and he regretted having denied them his horse, but he wasn't able to say no again, and much less repress a feeling of joy deep inside himself.

But when in the descent he felt Maddalena's soft breast pressing a little too much against his back, as in his dream, and her arm a little too tight around his waist, he, who believed in dreams, remembered his and sat up straight.

Carried by the strong horse through the twisting and turning on the heights and over paths hollowed out of rock and covered with flowering bushes, in minutes Elias and Maddalena found themselves alone, silent, wrapped tightly in their sad love. It was a moment in which Maddalena, of a passionate and weak nature, was unable to restrain herself.

'Elias,' she said in a slightly trembling voice, 'I'm sorry if I annoy you.'

'Oh!' he said, shaking his head.

'Next year you'll have your own wife on the back of your horse . . .'

'My wife?'

'Yes, Paska. Then you'll be happy.'

'And you won't be happy?'

'Oh, I'll be dead . . .'

'Dead! . . . Maddalena!'

'Dead . . . to life . . . to love, I mean . . .'

Not only did her voice tremble, but her hand, poised on Elias' belt, was also trembling, as was her whole body collapsed against his back. He was also vibrating like a broken string and a shadow veiled his eyes: it was the same anguish, the same rapture as his dream.

'Maddalena . . .' he murmured, squeezing her hand; but immediately he stiffened, and said aloud: 'I thought you were falling; sit straight, keep your balance.'

The words of Father Porcheddu echoed strongly, insistently in his soul; and his vow didn't leave his mind. 'Don't worry, Pietro, my brother; even if she throws herself at me, I'll push her away.'

Nuoro was near, down there behind the edge of the valley illuminated by the falling sun. The caravan stopped there on the height, on tired and sweating horses, the gold of the sky shining on the background, before going on together into the town and three times

64

around the little church of Rosario. Its bell was already ringing, far off, silvery, greeting the little saint's return.

IV

Here Elias is at last, in the boundless solitude of the *tanca*, enlivened only by a shout, a shepherd's whistle, the tinkling of the flocks and the lowing of the cows. Thick cork woods stand out against the horizon, touching the serene sky in the background. The Portolus' *tanca* had been cleared of trees years ago, and now lay open, vast, beaten by the sun. Here and there rose an occasional cork tree in the green grass, the scrub, the blackberry bushes; in the damp expanse the vegetation was tender and delicate, perfumed by mint and thyme. The luxuriant pastures took on a luminous golden green in the springtime. Thistles opened up their gold and violet flowers, the blackberries threw out their wild florets. Only under the trees and in the humid stretches did the grass stay green and fresh. The *tanca*, even if level and woodless, had secret recesses, rocks and scrub brush; water flowed in certain places through elder woods where the sun barely penetrated, forming mysterious little green lakes, surrounded and divided by rocks breaking the course of the murmuring water. In a wide area along the banks the vegetation stayed fresh and soft. At night the odour of reeds and mint was almost irritating. The Portolus' good-sized flock grazed in the *tanca*; the sheep were big with tangled fleece, the lambs large and fat. Within two or three days the flock had to be sheared. Elias felt physically well in that solitary, wildly beautiful place where he had grown up, where he had spent his early youth. Day after day he visited and recognized every corner, every recess of the *tanca*.

The dogs – one big, black and wild-eyed, reposing Olympianly under the tree he was chained to, the other small, with stiff reddish fur like a little pig – had recognized Elias; and he had nearly wept as he caressed them.

In addition to the dogs in the sheepfold there were a tame and mischievous piglet with bright, affectionate eyes that seemed human, a big black cat and a beautiful white kid goat that served as a guide for the sheep, happily showing the way when a difficult pass had to be crossed or a stream waded. When it was not grazing, the beautiful little kid stayed close to Mattia, following in his footsteps, running after him, jumping on him, showing its affection in a hundred ways. This little animal went into the hut, bothered the cat, played with the piglet or the little dog, and slept at Mattia's feet.

Life was primitive and simple in the Portolus'

sheepfold, frequented only by neighbouring shepherds or some passers-by. Suspicious characters, fugitives or other travellers didn't happen by there: Zio Portolu was an honest and industrious man, Mattia a little simple. Elias had no desire to get back in touch with old acquaintances or to make new ones.

Now he loved the solitude, and often during those first days spent in the sheepfold even avoided the company of his own family when his work didn't make it necessary. He wandered here and there, seeking out the places that reminded him of his childhood, often feeling affected. Anything could easily affect him, but after the first instinctive stirrings of his soul he became irritated by what he thought a weakness, so much more so if his brother, and especially Zio Portolu, should notice and laugh at him.

'Eh, eh, what are you?' Zio Portolu would ask him. 'You've turned into a man soft as fresh cheese, Elias, my son. You turn as pale as a silly woman over every little thing. Men must be men, lions; don't get emotional, don't make faces, don't cry. What is a man who cries? He's nothing. See your brother Mattia? He's not an eagle, and he's astonished about many things, but he certainly doesn't change colour; and at times his astonishment is also shrewdness; eh, don't look at Mattia like that. He's more cunning than you.'

After these little sermons, often repeated, Elias proposed to be shrewd and strong himself, but how? Certain thoughts, certain memories, certain feelings attacked him so suddenly that he was then no longer

68

master of himself, and he returned to feelings of tenderness, anger, shame.

He had brought with him all the books he owned, but they were not many: the book for Holy Week, some little religious books that had been distributed in *that place*. *The Battle of Benevento*, pamphlets of Sardinian poetry and an old illustrated herb book. He hid them in a very safe and sheltered place, under a rock in the elder wood, his favourite place to rest. But Zio Portolu and Mattia (who knew how to read) also had their books: [9] *French Royalty* and *Guerino, alias Meschino*, and even the *Little Flowers of Saint Francis*. How many times Mattia had read them to himself, to his father, to his shepherd friends! And what childlike emotions those strong men felt (who didn't want to be touched by other things) every time they read or listened to the adventures of Guerino or the words of *Little Flowers*.

Of all his books, Elias preferred the one for Holy Week. He already knew the Gospels by heart and could just about read them with ease in Latin, also. He would go into the coolness of the elder woods, into the shade fragrant with reeds, near the murmuring water, and read the holy words. At that time the work at the sheepfold was finished. Mattia would trot towards Nuoro on his horse followed by the colt, with his saddlebag full of fresh cheese and ricotta; Zio Portolu, sitting beside his hut, would patiently cut and carve a gourd, drawing an episode from the *Guerino* on it, muttering, talking to the gourd, to the penknife, to his fingers, to the ink he was using; and the flock took a siesta in the shade of the brushwood, and the pig, the goat, the cat and the dogs slept. The whole *tanca* rested in the burning sun under the clear metal sky, ashen-grey on the horizon; not a blade of glass would be stirring.

Elias reread his book, cradled by the murmuring water, but in that infinitive peace his heart was not tranquil. Often, in the middle of a line, a memory would flash through his mind, demanding all his attention. And that memory was not good – oh – it was not good, it was not good!

Sometimes he would go to sleep like that, in the deep quiet of noontime, and inevitably Maddalena would appear to him in a dream. And they were dreams that disturbed and excited him painfully, leaving him with a bad feeling for the rest of the day. He had hoped to calm himself and forget in the solitude of the *tanca*, far from her; but memories of those days spent at the church of St Francis, that dream on the banks of the Isalle, that fatal ride back home, were too recent. His blood was still burning, and his will alone could not put out the fire; the solitude, his recovering physical strength only increased his passion.

But above all it increased the fixed, insistent, indestructible memory of the ride back from the feast; Elias' dreams kept reviving that scene, so that his back, his waist, his hand preserved intact the physical impression of Maddalena's body and hands. And his mind, remembering her words, would be lost again in a swirl of pleasure and anguish.

He was angry with himself, but he had no control;

70

at times his lips would pronounce his vow and at the same time his thought would get lost there, in memories. Then he would cover himself with curses, want to beat and punish himself, but he found it impossible to control himself.

'My father is right,' he would think, 'I'm soft as fresh cheese, an animal, a fool. Why think about women, especially the one I mustn't look at? Can't you live without them? Men must be men, lions; and I'm a lamb, a dimwit of a sheep. But what can I do? I'm not made that way; if I were made like that I'd have a heart of stone. But, who knows, this madness may pass in time.'

His thinking went along those lines, but it was no comfort because he felt that that madness would last a long time.

At the same time a sharp desire to see Maddalena again grew stronger in his heart day by day; but there he held to his plan. But that wasn't all. He was dreading the day when Maddalena, Pietro and Zia Annedda would come for the sheep shearing; and yet he counted the hours that brought him closer to that day, and felt a quivering pleasure mixed with fear at its approach.

On the eve of that day he was closing a break in the wall of the *tanca*. Beyond it spread the woods guarded by Zio Martinu Monne, the Father of the Woods. Where was Zio Martinu? Elias still hadn't seen him, although he had looked for him three or four times.

Suddenly that evening here came Zio Martinu out of the woods heading for the wall. He was an old giant,

71

still straight and strong, with long yellowish hair and a thick grey beard; his face creased in deep wrinkles seemed cast in bronze. He was majestic in his dark costume and sleeveless overjacket of oiled leather; he seemed like a prehistoric man. Elias gave a cry of joy, vaulted the wall, took the old man's hand.

'How lucky to see you, Zio Martinu! I've looked for you many times; how are you?'

'How nice to see you! And one hundred years before another misfortune like the one just passed. How are you? I'm fine. I had to be away for a few days,' answered Zio Martinu calmly, in a strong voice, pronouncing his words slowly.

They sat on the wall and talked at length, telling each other many things.

'The first day I got back,' Elias then said, 'I dreamed about you. I was in our courtyard at home, I was tired and had a little to drink and went to sleep. And I dreamed of you: we were like this, like we are now, in front of this wall. Dreams do come true!'

'Oh?' the other said, but without surprise.

Elias didn't tell him about the dream in detail, but asked: 'Do you believe in dreams?'

'What do you want me to say? Dreams don't really come true, but it often happens that we anticipate a thing, think of it a good deal, and then dream about it; afterwards it happens; to us it seems like the dream came true, but it was something that simply had to happen.'

Once again Elias admired Zio Martinu's wisdom, but shook his head. He was thinking about the dream on the banks of the Isalle. Had he anticipated and perhaps desired the talk he had later with Maddalena? No, it didn't seem like that to him.

'Tomorrow,' he said after a moment, 'tomorrow we shear the sheep, Zio Martinu. You're coming, aren't you? My mother will be here, my brother Pietro and his fiancée.'

'Ah, yes, I heard your brother is engaged. Is she a good woman?'

'Yes, she seems good. She's beautiful.'

'Eh, that isn't enough. Paintings are beautiful, you put them on the wall and they only serve as decoration. A woman must be good, affectionate to her husband, and not love any other man on this earth.'

Elias grew pensive and didn't reply. Besides it was getting late, the sky was growing pale, the woods were silent in the solemn quiet of the evening. He must go back to the hut.

'Will you come, Zio Martinu? We'll be expecting you, don't forget.'

'I'll come.'

'Don't forget,' warned Elias, jumping over the wall.

'I've always kept my word, Elias Portolu. Give your father my greetings.'

'Indeed. Good evening.'

'Good evening.'

Zio Martinu didn't forget, and in fact he came very early to help the shepherds in the preparations for this country festival. The orange-coloured dawn burned in the east, pouring a splendour of rose-gold on the grass and rocks of the *tanca*; to the west the woods were silent against the clear slate background of the sky.

Zio Portolu heated a rock red hot to make junket. Elias and Zio Martinu killed a lamb as big as a sheep. They skinned it, quartered it, and extracted the smoking entrails.

A little after sunrise Pietro and the women arrived. They came slowly in a cart led by Pietro; no one made a move to meet them, but Elias felt his heart beating violently. Maddalena alighted first, agile and quick, gave her clothes a shake and helped her mother and Zia Annedda down.

While Pietro unloaded the cart (Zia Annedda had brought bread and wine in abundance), the women went toward the hut; Maddalena was fresher and more graceful than ever; her dazzling white blouse, embroidered and starched, and her skirt of dark calico with the border of blue emphasized her beautiful shape. As soon as he saw her close by and was under the sway of those burning eyes, Elias felt lost.

But in that confusion of anxious pleasure he had the strength to think: 'I mustn't be alone with her, otherwise I'm a lost man. I've got to tell someone to follow me always and never leave me alone with her, if that possibility arises. Ah, I'm afraid of myself. But who can I tell? My mother? My father? No, no it's not possible. Mattia? He wouldn't understand. Ah, Zio Martinu!'

He took a deep breath. Zio Martinu in the meantime was solemnly looking down at the fiancée, while Zio Portolu made the introductions, laughing with his forced, caustic laugh.

74

'Eh, eh, whitehaired old boar, see Pietro's bride? Her name is Maddalena, and she knows how to spin and sew, and no one has ever said anything against her. Look at her, the white dove; don't you smell the perfume of roses? And this is Arrita Scada, the old dove, see her, Martinu Monne?'

'I see her.'

'Good day,' said Zia Arrita, turning to the old man curiously. 'You're from Orune, aren't you? Are you staying on someone's *tanca*?'

'I am from Orune, and I'm staying on someone's *tanca*.'

'You can talk later!' shouted Zio Portolu. 'Now let's drink the junket and eat the curdled milk. Let's go, hurry up, let's go!'

'The sun has hardly come up; it's not time to drink junket,' Maddalena said laughing.

'My daughter,' pontificated Zia Arrita, 'we must eat and drink when they invite us, whether the sun is high or low.'

'Eh, eh, Martinu Monne, hear the old dove? Didn't I tell you she's as wise as water?'

They went into the hut where Mattia was with the goat on one side and the cat on the other; then Pietro arrived and the picture was complete. The women sat on the cork stools, Elias, silent but not sad, handed out the spoons made of a sheep's hoof, and Zio Portolu uncorked the jars full of junket and milk. Zio Martinu dominated the scene and didn't take his eyes off Maddalena. They ate and drank copiously; the junket was exquisite, and Zio Portolu would have been offended if the guests had not drunk it all.

Immediately after breakfast the shearing began; the sheep were caught, tied, stretched out on the grass without their putting up the slightest resistance; Mattia and Elias sheared them skilfully with large shears. Tangled, dirty wool piled up here and there on the ground and, freed from the lasso, the sheep – smaller now, tranquil – went back to grazing.

The women prepared lunch, as usual, leaving the carving of the lamb to Zio Portolu; however, Maddalena obstinately followed Elias as though drawn by a magic thread, and every time he raised his eyes he met hers that seemed to want to bewitch him. Suddenly they were alone. Pietro had gone to the hut, Mattia was chasing a lamb more restless than the others and Zio Martinu went to help him.

Elias had a moment of confusion, of fear, of indescribable pleasure at finding himself alone with Maddalena; alone, amidst the grasses and high flowering thistle. His heart pounded and dizzy desire whirled throughout his being when his eyes met those passionate and pleading eyes of Maddalena.

'Save me! Save us!' that look said to him. 'You love me, I love you, I have come to ask you to save me and save us. Elias, Elias!'

But he thought he would lose himself and lose her if he just kept looking at her. He did violence to himself; he looked away. The sheep ran through the grass, followed by Zio Martinu and Mattia who were trying to push it into a bush.

'How stupid!' Elias said. 'If I had gone it would be sheared by now.'

And he dashed off, leaving Maddalena alone in the sun, in the grass and tall flowering thistle; alone with the eyes of a Madonna lowered in sorrowful resignation.

'Zio Martinu,' Elias said to the old man, while Mattia went ahead of them pulling the reluctant sheep, 'do me a favour, Zio Martinu, don't leave me alone for a moment with that girl.'

He spoke softly, a little anxious, a little ashamed, with eyes downcast. Zio Martinu gazed intently at him from above for a long moment. He understood, not saying a word in reply.

'I'll tell you . . . this evening . . . It's nothing bad, Zio Martinu,' Elias said raising his eyes. 'I trust you more than my father.'

Zio Martinu didn't answer, wasn't affected, didn't smile; he only clapped Elias on the shoulder, and for the entire day followed him around like a shadow.

Dinner was noisy and happy beyond words. Zio Portolu announced to Zio Martinu that Madallena and Prededdu would be married soon, after harvest; but the old man didn't seem overjoyed at this news.

The women and Pietro left towards sunset; Maddalena seemed happy. Laughing and joking she continually smiled at Pietro and paid no more attention to Elias. But Elias, urged on a bit by his own ego, wasn't taken in by her false gaiety.

'She'll think I'm stupid,' he thought. 'Oh, well, so much the better; but if she only knew . . . if she knew . . .'

It seemed as though his heart would break at any moment, and he had the insane desire to sob out loud, to shout, to beat his head. In the meanwhile the cart was going away, and the red of the women's bodices and the black and white figure of Pietro disappeared down there, in the green depths of the *tanca*, in the rose-coloured sunset. Farewell, farewell. He would never again see her that way, free and in love, in the solitude of the *tanca*, throbbing with love next to him as on that spring morning. Everything was finished.

The cart disappeared in the distance and everything was silent, everything was empty around Elias. But turning to go back to the hut, he saw Zio Martinu waiting for him.

'I'm going,' the old man said. 'Do you want to come with me, Elias?'

'Let's go.'

The sun had set, and the woods and distance were silent under the rose-coloured sky – a dense, almost violent rosiness; the whole *tanca*, the shining bushes, the still grass, the rocks and water reflected that luminosity of pink peonies. It was a near-religious peace, like a church illuminated by burning candles. Zio Martinu and Elias silently crossed the *tanca*, and went to sit on the wall, serious and thoughtful.

Elias felt sad; he didn't know how to begin, and looked stubbornly at his hands; Zio Martinu understood his young friend's state of mind and tried to save him embarrassment.

'Elias Portolu,' he said gravely, 'I know what you want to tell me. Maddalena is in love with you.'

'Quiet!' said the other, frightened, putting his hand on his arm. 'Every little bush has ears!'[10] he then added to explain his distress.

'Yes,' replied the Father of the Woods, in a serious voice, 'every little bush, every tree, every stone has ears. And what of it? What I said and what I'm going to say anyone can hear, beginning with God who is up there, and ending with the lowliest servant. Maria Maddalena loves you, you love her; unite yourselves in God, because he created you for one another.'

Elias looked at him dazed; he was remembering his talk with Father Porcheddu, the advice, the warnings on that unforgettable night at St Francis. Who should he listen to?

'But she is to be the bride of my brother, Zio Martinu!'

'And what if she is to be the bride of your brother? Does she love him? No. So she isn't his and will never be his according to the laws of the Lord. The marriage of love is the marriage of God; the marriage of convenience is the marriage of the devil. Save yourself, Elias Portolu, and save the dove, as your father calls her. Maria Maddalena accepted Pietro because he imposed himself on her, because he had wheat, because he had barley, beans, a house, oxen, land. The devil was at work. But God had other plans. He ordained your return, your meeting with the girl. You saw each other, you fell in love, even while knowing that men's prejudices would not permit you even to look at one another. Don't you feel in this a force greater than man, pointing out His way? Isn't it God's

79

hand? Think it over well, Elias Portolu; think about it – have you thought about it?'

'It's true. But Pietro is my brother.'

'We are all brothers, Elias Portolu. Pietro is not stupid, he understands reason. Go, tell him: "Brother, I love your fiancée and she loves me; what are you going to do? Do you want to make your brother and that other innocent creature unhappy?"'

Elias felt cold just at the thought of talking to his brother like that, and he shook his head in sorrow and dread.

'Never! Never! Pietro would kill me, Zio Martinu!'

'In my opinion you're afraid.'

'Yes, why hide it from you? I'm afraid, but not of death. It's because Maddalena would be lost and Pietro too, and my whole family. But that's not the only thorn in my heart, Zio Martinu. I love my brother and don't want him to be unhappy, even though he might be resigned.'

'Pietro could resign himself more easily than you; he has a different character from you. I understand your good sentiments, Elias Portolu, but I don't approve of them. Think of the consequences; have you ever thought of those? Maddalena loves you desperately, I've read it in her eyes. If you keep quiet, she will marry Pietro, she will come to live in your house, and you will end by losing yourself since human nature is fragile. Are you listening, Elias Portolu? Have you ever thought of that? Temptation can be conquered today, tomorrow, but the day after tomorrow it will

80

end by conquering you, because we are not made of stone. Have you thought of that, Elias Portolu?'

'It's true! It's true!' Elias said, his eyes filled with dread.

They were silent a moment. About them the silence was intense, infinite; dusk fell on the woods, the peony sky faded into tender shades of violet. And suddenly Elias felt that great mysterious peace penetrate his heart.

'But I,' he said with a changed voice, 'I'll go along home.'

'You will take a wife? Careful that that won't make it worse.'

'No, I'll never take a wife.'

'What will you do, then?'

'I'll become a priest. You aren't surprised, Zio Martinu?'

'Nothing surprises me.'

'What do you advise me to do now? In the dream I told you about, that I had on the first night I came back, you advised me to become a priest.'

'A dream is one thing, reality another, Elias Portolu. I don't advise against it if you have a vocation, but I'll say that not even that will save you. We are men, Elias, men fragile as cane; give it careful thought.'

'What do you advise me to do, then?'

'I've already given you my advice. Go to town, talk to your brother.'

'Never . . . never . . . with him!'

'Well, then, talk to your mother. Your mother is a

holy woman. She will put a soothing balm on every wound.'

'All right then, yes, I'll go!' Elias said with sudden energy.

It was decided, and joy flashed in his eyes. He stood up, took a few steps; he wanted to leave immediately, free himself immediately from the nightmare that was crushing him. It all seemed easy, the best thing to do; and for a few moments he felt as intense a happiness as he had ever felt in his life.

'All right, don't waste time,' Zio Martinu said to him. 'Go tomorrow, speak, don't have scruples or reservations. I'll be here tomorrow at this time; you can tell me what you've done.'

'I'll go and come back tomorrow, Zio Martinu. Good night, and thanks, Zio Martinu.'

'Good night, Elias Portolu.'

And each went his own way.

The next day, at the same time, the two men met in the same place, near the wall of the *tanca*. All around was the same pure, infinite silence; the sunset lit the tops of the woods, a magpie sang in the distance; but Elias was sad, undone, with his face suffused with tiredness and suffering as on the first days after his return.

'Zio Martinu,' he said, 'if you knew how it all went! It's useless, I can't, I can't speak – not to my mother, not to anyone. Last night I felt sure, I seemed to have the heart of a lion; more, nerves like steel. Well, then I lay down and slept and in my dream I thought I was home talking to my mother . . . It all seemed easy. I

82

woke up, left, went home. And all the time I was happy, full of hope and courage. I called my mother aside and felt the words I had prepared come to my lips. She looked at me and suddenly I felt my heart pounding and a knot closed my throat. Ah, no, Zio Martinu, it's impossible, I can't speak, even if I wanted to. I could commit a crime, but reveal *that thing* to my family, no. It's impossible.'

'Try again,' the old man said. But Elias made a gesture of revulsion, almost of disgust.

'Ah, no!' he said in a loud voice. 'Don't tempt me, Zio Martinu; I don't have the courage to do it. I could go a thousand times and not be able to do it.'

'That's true,' the old man said, and seemed struck by a memory. 'I forget something that happened,' he added after a little. 'It was really even more serious, but the man was also stronger than you, courageous, daring, violent. He had to commit a crime (and he had already committed others); he had to kill an honest man. It seemed a natural, very simple thing to him, very easy, and in his heart he was more than ready. The day arrived, the designated hour. He went to the honest man's house, found him at supper, could have killed him without any danger. But the honest man looked at him and this was enough to make the other unable to raise his arm. And this happened two, three, ten times.'

While the old man was talking, Elias devoured him with his eyes, forgetting his torment as he listened to the story. Ah, he already knew that story, not only that but he knew that the violent man was Zio

Martinu himself. Besides, everyone had known that story for years, and they added that the honest man, after getting to know him, called Zio Martinu and gave him work. He made him his shepherd and then custodian of his *tancas*. From then on Zio Martinu had become his right arm, the most faithful servant of the man he had wanted to kill.

Elias felt a sense of relief; deep down he was ashamed of his weakness and continual indecision; but if a man of iron like Zio Martinu Monne in his wild youth was unable to overcome the power of one honest look, how could he, poor weak boy, overcome the dread of confessing to his family what seemed like a crime to him?

'The story that I've told you,' the old man added, 'certainly doesn't compare with yours, but just the same it does show how there is a power over us that we can't defeat. Nevertheless, if you can Elias, try to do something!'

'I can't do anything, Zio Martinu!' said a discouraged Elias.

'Perhaps you would like me to intercede . . .' the old man began, thoughtfully, after a brief silence; but Elias squeezed his arm and protested loudly.

'Never, Zio Martinu! Never, never! Ah, don't do me the wrong of believing I had even thought of that. Not only that, Zio Martinu, but if you tell my secret, I'll never look you in the face again.'

'You are right; that's not the way. True!'

'Then what do you advise?'

'I've already advised you, Elias Portolu. Do

84

something, stir yourself, be provident.'

'I am provident, Zio Martinu. I'll let things take their course. Then, if I can't hold out, I'll do what we talked about last evening.'

'And you will do badly,' said the old man rising. 'Try your best, Elias, my son; the story that I told you ended well because of the man's indecision; but you will end badly. You know how to write; well then, write, since your brother knows how to read. Come to an understanding, look to the future. I have no more to say.'

A light of hope flashed again in Elias' eyes.

'Yes, I'll write.'

They separated without setting another time to meet, and Elias went to the hut with his heart a little lighter. 'Yes, yes,' he repeated to himself, 'I'll write to Pietro like gentlemen do; I'll tell him everything, and he is reasonable and will listen. I have pen and paper; I'll give the letter to Mattia . . . no, I'll take it myself, I'll give it to my mother to put in the proper hands. Yes, all right.'

For long hours during the night he thought over how to write the letter; he already knew how to start it and how to finish it; the rest was easy. The following morning he awoke still firm in his resolution; as soon as he could he went to his favourite place where he had hidden his books and pen and a small section of cane full of ink, and he prepared everything. He sat next to a high rock, finding the right position – the best position for writing in comfort; then he lapsed into thought.

The brook nearby murmured among the reeds; a pleasant breeze snaked through the elder trees and the tall grass made long rustling sounds. Vague, muffled sounds near and far animated the *tanca* under the light blue luminosity of pure morning.

Elias was thinking, with his hands (no longer white) firm on the sheet of ordinary paper before him on the rock. Suddenly he raised his head, as though listening to a distant voice; then he took the paper, the pen, the ink, put it all back in the hiding place, and went back to the hut. He was unable to conquer the great power that Zio Martinu had talked about.

V

Summer arrived. The entire *tanca* turned a beautiful pale yellow, except in the brush along the banks of the brook where the vegetation took on a tropical luxuriance. What a sweet sight there in the resplendent mornings, in the twilights of rosy-gold, in the nights brilliant with the purest stars when the new moon rose mysteriously over the silent woods!

Elias was worn out from love and sadness, but he didn't make a plan or a move that might stop the event. In the meanwhile time was passing; Pietro had an exceptional harvest, and the wedding would take place in a few days. Elias hadn't seen Zio Martinu again, and he didn't try to see him; he was almost afraid of him, because instead of comforting him, the old man – who was considered very wise – had put his soul in hell.

'And if he should be right?' Elias sometimes asked

87

himself; but he soon rebelled at this thought, because he didn't feel he had the strength to act, to move, to give away his secret, and above all to cross Pietro's happiness.

But the memory of and desire for Maddalena and the thought that soon she would be irrevocably lost to him was consuming him. He tried to fight his heart and senses, to laugh at his passion, to be strong like Zio Portolu wanted; what the devil! there were lots of women in the world; and besides you can even live without them, even without love; and so a man who is really a man must laugh at these things!

But the fight was useless. Without the figure of Maddalena on Elias' horizon it was entirely bleak and dark. And so, just as he had ardently yearned for the remoteness, solitude and silence of the *tanca* when he was at the church of St Francis, now he yearned for Pietro's wedding day. At least then everything would be over, forever. It seemed to him that *afterwards* he would heal, finding once again peace and health. Because he felt himself deteriorating physically also. The heat of those long, luminous days and the insidious coolness of the clear perfumed nights were destroying him and making him feverish.

In his sadness he had come to hate men; even his father and Mattia disgusted him, and so he avoided them. He wandered all day across the yellow, burning solitude of the *tanca*, and spent nights in the open air.

If he slept at noon, after reading and rereading his holy books, he would wake up with his head wrapped in pain; and after that he couldn't sleep at night. Then he would stay hidden for a long time, crouched over the rocks to watch the moon go down over the woods, or be immersed in a sorrowful languor. Zio Portolu, the old fox, saw clearly the state of his son's mind and body without being able to guess the cause. It grieved him and he would shout bitterly at Elias during the few minutes they were together.

'Why do you hide?' he would shout. 'What kind of life is that? If you are planning a crime, do it and get it over with; if you are in love, do something about it. Are you a man? You are a twig, a little cow made of cheese! Don't you see you can't stand on your two legs, and that your face is as green as a frog's?'

'I'm not well,' Elias said, not to make excuses but because he had a foolish fear that Zio Portolu would guess his secret.

'If you're sick, get well or die; I don't want to see weak people around me, I want to see lions, I want to see eagles, and you are a lizard.'

'Leave me in peace, papa,' Elias begged, moving away in annoyance.

'Go to the devil! Go to the devil!' Zio Portolu yelled after him; but when he was alone the old man grew sad – he too felt weak-hearted as a little bird.

'Stay to watch Elias get sick. Ah, no, St Francis mine – take me, but keep my sons alive and strong! My sons! My doves! My little birds! Ah, may they be happy and Zio Portolu die in despair. Elias, Elias, why don't you get well? What will I do without you? I'll get your mother to come, I'll make you go back to town with her; she'll put you to bed and give you that medicine she knows how to make, with herbs, salt and holy medallions.

Meanwhile Elias wandered around, sad, desperate, aggravated with himself and others. One night Zio Portolu, while crossing the *tanca*, saw him perched on a rock, contemplating the moon.

'What secret thing is he up to? Planning a crime? Thinking of becoming a priest?' the old man asked himself, looking at his son with eyes redder than usual from the heat of that dazzling day. 'My St Francis, *Santu Franzischeddu meu*, heal this dear boy.'

He returned to the hut very distressed. Oh, indeed, Elias' strange behaviour was poisoning his joy in Pietro's wedding that would be celebrated on Sunday.

Meanwhile Elias, on top of the rock, with his vitreous eyes fixed as though enchanted by the pure splendour of the moon, was unmoving, immersed in a confusion of visions. He felt the same bewilderment, the buzzing, the vague dizziness that he had felt in the family courtyard on the evening of his return. The light breeze that rustled in the woods far away seemed an incoherent voice, now sweet, now frightening. What was it saying? What was the wind saying? What were the woods murmuring? He would have liked to hear that voice distinctly, and it grieved him, moved him, irritated him not to be able to. It seemed like the voice of Father Porcheddu, of Maddalena, of his mother, of Zio Martinu; he remembered the dream he had on the first evening of his return and the one on the banks of the Isalle, and other long-ago dreams and visions. And he felt a confused torment in the depths of his soul over that voice he couldn't hear and for those dreams, and for other things he couldn't remember.

The moon shone on his face, on his eyes, casting over him the enchantment of a dream. All around, along the line of the woods, on the distant horizon, the sky faded into a pearly splendour. The flock was still grazing in the distance, the melancholy tinkling of their bells filling the nocturnal solitude. But Elias felt as sad as on that other night. An unusual thing happened also; that is, he remembered the days, the months, the years passed in *that place*; he remembered them with humiliating sorrow, as he had never remembered them; and confusedly he was thinking: 'Ah, if I had not sinned or kept bad company, I wouldn't have been in *that place*, I would have known Maddalena before Pietro, and I wouldn't be so unhappy now. They tamed me, it's true, and they made me as weak as a woman. And to say that I always talk about my memories of *that place* and am proud of them! Shame, Elias Portolu, shame!'

And he felt his face flush, and again his thoughts were a jumble. The visions and mixed voices returned, as well as the figures of Father Porcheddu, Maddalena, Zio Martinu, and those he had seen in *that place*. And the anguish that weighed on his heart became heavier every hour, crushing him like a boulder. Finally he seemed to grab hold of the illusive memory and hear the voice: a shudder went through him and his face turned livid, his teeth chattered.

'In three days she'll be married: it's all finished!' he

91

shouted to himself. 'That's what is killing me, and I don't do anything, I don't move, I don't dare . . .'

A desperate impulse seized him, a madness of rash plans.

'I'm going home, I'll do something. I don't want to die. I love her and she loves me, she told me down there, on the banks of the Isalle . . . no, while we were coming back . . . anyway, she told me, and I kissed her, and she is mine, mine, mine . . . I'll go . . . Ah, brother mine, kill me if you want to, but she's mine. Now I'll go down, I'll run, I'll go to Nuoro and settle everything. Everything can be settled; Zio Martinu is right; but it has to be done quickly.'

He moved; soon cold shivers assailed him, starting from his feet and snaking up through his whole body; he sat down again facing the moon, with his face ashen, his teeth chattering. He was remembering his vow the evening he had cried like a baby at the feet of St Francis; but by now those intentions were far away. He seemed to be overcome by passion and unable to fight it.

He thought: 'At that time it seemed the wedding day would never arrive. Now it's near, the day after tomorrow. I have to get moving.'

'But why can't I move?' he asked himself, in a moment of lucidity. 'I try to move and I can't. My legs feel as heavy as stone. And this shivering? I have a fever, I must be getting sick.'

'Ah,' he thought with terror, 'and if I get ill? If I can't move? And in the meanwhile . . . Ah, no, no, I'm going, I'm going.'

He stood up heavily, got off the rock and staggered along, across the stubble and sparkling hay that sent out its perfume under the moon.

He heard the melancholy tinkling of the flock. He wanted to run, but he couldn't, and every once in a while he stopped with a heavy buzzing and sharp whistling in his ears.

Suddenly he fell on the ground under a tree, through whose limbs he saw the moon looking at him with a bright, almost sparkling eye. That eye of the moon was his last impression; after that he felt only a sharp pain over his left eyebrow, as if someone had struck him with an axe; and the buzzing in his ears grew. But in his evil dream he continued walking, saying the strangest things. He seemed to cross a place full of monstrous rocks, spiny bushes, dry thistles, illuminated by a bluish moonlight.

In his delirium he remembered perfectly where he was heading and what he wanted; but although he was running, climbing over rocks, jumping bushes, sweating, struggling, he wasn't able to get out of *that place*. And he felt an indescribable anger and pain. All his joints ached, he felt as if his back was broken, his feet, hands, temples pulsed, and his whole body was covered with sweat; but he kept on going, up through those rocks that gave him a sense of fear, a sense of horror, in that livid brightness of an invisible moon that surrounded him with a strange light sadder and more frightening than the dark. How long that tremendous battle lasted with the rocks, bushes, thistles, with his undefined anger, with his oppressive

93

pain, with his fear of invisible monsters, with the horrible, unspecific light, he never knew. Other visions no less monstrous, but confused, insistent, that intertwined, dissolved, returned like clouds blown by the wind, enveloped him, tormented him.

The moment came at last when his mind, tired and defeated, sank into the dark abyss of unconsciousness, while his body continued to suffer; then, like a sad dawn, light descended into the abyss and gradually grew until his mind became aware of his body's suffering, but no longer in a dream, and he feverishly opened his eyes to reality.

He was in his own house, in his bed with the rough wool blanket, in his humble little white bedroom. A melancholy twilight shone through the half-closed window. From the lane came the happy cries of children, and from the courtyard, kitchen, the next rooms came the sound of subdued voices. There must be a great number of people. What were they saying? What were they doing? Was Maddalena there? And Pietro? Were they married?

Elias felt very cold; but now the delirium had passed, and even if Maddalena were not married and came to him, he wouldn't say anything. And indeed he hoped the wedding had already taken place, but with this hope a violent sadness gripped him so powerfully he cried out for death.

But instead of death life returned, the anxieties returned. Had he talked in his delirium? What had happened? How had they found him? How had they brought him back? Had Maddalena seen him? Had

94

Maddalena felt sorry for him? At the notion of her pitying him he felt moved, desiring once again to die.

At that moment Zia Annedda entered. She noticed Elias' improvement at once and bent over his pillow smiling with joy and compassion.

'Does she know?' Elias asked, lowering his dark eyelids.

'My son, how do you feel?' his mother asked, putting her hand on his forehead.

'So-so.'

'God be blessed. You had a high fever, Elias. The wedding was nearly postponed . . .'

'She knows!' he thought sorrowfully.

'But this morning you were already a little better. Your brother was married at ten.'

'They don't know anything!'

But this thought was not enough to relieve him from the unspeakable sorrow that his mother's words had given him. Because in the end he had still hoped. What had he hoped for? He didn't even know himself; he had hoped for the unknown, the impossible, but he had hoped.

Now it was all over. He closed his eyes and didn't open his mouth again and heard his mother no longer. His entire body felt numb and heavy, immovable as a rock, and it seemed to him that even if he wanted to move he couldn't.

It was all over.

Zia Annedda left him alone again; as she opened the door, Elias heard more distinctly the voices and subdued laughter coming from the kitchen and courtyard. He opened his eyes again, looked at the walls where the melancholy brightness of the twilight was dying. He thought of the joy of others who took no trouble over him, and felt more deeply his strong sorrow, his solitude, his end. And he silently wept, losing himself in a grief darker than death.

In the meantime the news of his improvement, passed around by Zia Annedda, removed the shadow that Elias' sickness had cast over the family and few guests, all of whom were relatives. Naturally the happiest person was Zio Portolu.

'St Francis be praised,' he said jumping to his feet. 'If my little boy died I couldn't survive it. Let's go to see him and keep him company; let's go.'

Because of his sadness he hadn't even drunk anything, and hadn't even made the four braids of hair; but he was clean, with his boots oiled with tallow, his costume brand new. Only Maddalena seemed to be indifferent, with her wide Madonna eyes lowered in resignation. She was sitting next to the groom in the courtyard and seldom spoke, looking at her rings and often changing them from one finger to another. Pietro was happy; his face was cleanshaven, his eyes shining, his lips red; and in his wedding suit – the embroidered collar of his white shirt folded back over the deep blue velvet waistcoat – he seemed almost handsome.

'Let's go, let's go,' Zio Portolu said, anxious to see Elias. And as soon as he opened the door of the little room he began joking, laughing with his forced laugh, without noticing the mortal grief that paralysed his son.

'You see the beautiful man, the little flower of our house, who wanted to die right on the day his brother was married? Is that the thing to do? Eh, but I saw you on the rock the other evening and I said to myself; the dove is getting sick. Then we found him there under the tree like a dead man, and we had to bring him in a cart. If that is the thing to do! Ah, your face was as white as ashes, Elias, ha, ha, you want something to drink? Ha, ha, wine cures all ills. You know your brother is married? Get up, then, and let's drink to the couple's health.'

'Leave him in peace,' Zia Annedda said in a low voice, pulling at his coat tail. And he became silent, gazing sadly at Elias' closed eyes.

The couple had stayed in the courtyard, surrounded by relatives. The conversation was not very lively; they still felt a heaviness around them, an uneasiness that the timid, cool manner of the bride did nothing to dissipate.

An insolent little urchin came up to the door asking loudly for sweets and throwing rocks at the wall. The bride's mother and another relative prepared supper. Zia Annedda, white-faced and calm, went on tiptoe back and forth from the courtyard to the kitchen, from the kitchen to Elias' bedroom. That Elias would get better she already knew. Believing that he had 'had a fright' she had prepared him a special drink, then had hung a holy medal around his neck, lighted a lamp to St Francis and finally said the magic *parole verdi*[11] to find out if he would live or die. They had replied that he would live; St Francis be praised and God be blessed in all His holy will.

Little by little the people went away; only the brother and sister and mother of the bride remained, and an old friend of Zia Annedda's. Supper was more melancholy than the wedding dinner; Elias could be heard groaning from time to time, and a veil of sadness hung over everyone.

'It seems like a funeral supper,' said Zio Portolu, forcing himself to laugh, but he felt sad and the melancholy that had veiled the wedding day seemed like an evil omen for the couple. When she was assured that everything was on the table, Zia Annedda went to Elias, bringing him a bowl of broth.

'Sit up a little and drink my son,' she said lovingly, cooling the broth with the spoon.

But Elias made a grimace of disgust and pushed his mother's hand away.

'Elias, my son, drink, be good; drink so you will get well.'

'No, no, no . . .' he repeated in a childish whine.

'Come on, be good. If you keep this up you'll really get sick, and it will be a mortal sin, because the Lord wants us to take care of our health.'

He opened two large eyes full of anguish and physical suffering.

'Leave me in peace, let me die in peace,' he said.

Zia Annedda went away and came back with Maddalena behind her. As soon as he saw the bride Elias began to tremble visibly, and he had neither the

98

desire nor the strength to hide his distress. He only tried to murmur his best wishes.

'Good luck . . .' but the words died in his throat.

'Elias, why are you acting like this? Why don't you drink something?' Maddalena said, cold and firm. 'You aren't a little boy. Why make your mother unhappy? Come on, be good, as she says.'

He sat up at once, took the bowl and drank, panting and trembling like a leaf. Afterwards they made him drink some wine, and he soon drifted into a light, pleasant drowsiness that turned into tranquil sleep.

But in the middle of the night he awoke, and as soon as awake, in spite of the physical well-being that the sleep had given him, he felt a rush of unspeakable distress, a profound desperation. Maddalena was there, under the same roof, and Pietro was happy.

Elias felt that for him, if the joy of life had ended, the struggle against pangs of jealousy, sin and sorrow was just beginning. Inside and outside of him loomed a terrible darkness. And he still felt the insane need to get up, to move, to walk, to go far away. That was his destiny.

'I will go,' he thought, 'I must go, must move, must go far away and never return. Otherwise I am lost. Ah, ah . . .'

Twisting and writhing, he clenched his fists and beat his head on his pillow, biting his lips to smother the sobs and groans, with the furious desire to tear out his heart, take it in his fist and smash it against the wall.

VI

Autumn came, bringing a sweet melancholy to the *tanca*. On these hazy days the landscape seemed more vast, with mysterious frontiers beyond the veiled limits of the horizon; and a more intense solitude weighed on the *tanca*; trees, rocks, bushes, took on a gravity as if they also felt the autumnal sadness. Slowly and mournfully great crows ploughed the pallid sky; autumnal grass was reborn in the stubble darkened by recent heavy rains.

On one of those veiled, still-warm days, Elias was sitting alone by the hut. As usual he was reading one of his little books of prayer and meditation. The flock was grazing far away; some graceful little autumn lambs, white as snow, bleated like spoiled children.

Elias was reading and waiting for Zio Martinu Monne. He had sent for him to ask his advice.

'This time,' he thought, 'this time I want to follow

the old man's advice. He has experience in life, and I probably would have done better to follow his advice from the first. That's that,' he concluded to himself with a sigh. 'Now it's all finished.'

Finally the great figure of the old man appeared out of the vaporous path, heading stiff and straight towards the hut.

Elias jumped to his feet, put down the little book and went to meet Zio Martinu. Even though he knew the *tanca* was deserted, remembering every little bush has ears as the proverb said, and wanting to speak freely, he led the old man to an open area without bushes or boulders. Only some rocks were in the stubble, and Elias and the old man sat down on two of them.

They began by talking about unimportant things; about what Zio Martinu had been doing since they had last seen each other, about the sheep, the lambs, a bull that had been stolen from a nearby *tanca*. But all at once the old man gazed at Elias and changed his tone.

'Why did you send for me, Elias Portolu? What is it?'

Elias shook, blushed and looked around. He didn't see anyone; the woods, the rocks, the shrubs lay silent in the misty background, under the torpor of the veiled sky.

'I want to ask your advice, Zio Martinu . . .'

'You've asked my advice at other times and you haven't followed it.'

'Now it's different, Zio Martinu. And perhaps it

101

would have been better to follow your advice at that time. But that's that, it's all over now. I want to become a priest, Zio Martinu. What do you say?'

The old man gazed thoughtfully into the distance.

'Are you still in love?'

'More than ever!' Elias burst out. And gradually his voice became weak, plaintive, almost a cry. 'Sometimes I think I'm going crazy. She's beautiful; oh, if you could see how beautiful she is now! I always vow not to go back home, not to see her, not to look at her, but the devil pushes me, my Zio Martinu; and she looks at me too and I'm afraid. I have to find a remedy; otherwise what you said will happen.'

'Why don't you get married?'

'Ah, don't talk to me about that!' Elias said, assuming an expression of disgust. 'I would mistreat her, I feel it, I might become bad, and the devil would have a greater hold on me.'

'And so Maria Maddalena looks at you?'

'Ah, don't say her name, Zio Martinu! Yes, she looks at me!'

'Then she's not an honest woman?'

'I think she's an honest woman, but she doesn't love her husband, has never loved him, and her husband doesn't treat her well. He soon got bored, Zio Martinu; and he often gets drunk and mean. They often quarrel.'

'So soon?'

'Oh, they began doing that right away. But just because she doesn't love him, I'm afraid Pietro will end up beating her. He doesn't want her to go out of

102

the house, to visit her mother, to talk to the neighbours.'

'Is he jealous?'

'No, he's not jealous – he never has been, but he's quick-tempered, drinks too much, doesn't take advantage of his good fortune.'

'Ah, Elias, Elias! What did I tell you? If only you had followed my advice!' the old man exclaimed; but immediately he shook his head and added, 'Anyway, who knows? It might have been the same thing for you.'

'Oh, no! What are you saying?' Elias said with fervour, while a painful dream shone in his eyes. 'I would have adored her thoughts, her desires . . .'

'Forget it! We talk like that, but the day comes when we get tired of everything, especially women. Do you believe, Elias Portolu, that this whim of yours would last long? The time will come when you'll laugh about it. She'll have children, she'll lose her looks, she won't look at you any more, she'll become like so many other mothers of families in the town – with dirty dresses, old, slovenly, ugly.'

'You're mistaken, Zio Martinu. That's the problem: she'll never have children, she'll keep her beauty and freshness for a long time.'

'What do you know about it, Elias Portolu?'

'My mother, who understands these things, told me. I believe that's the reason for Pietro's bad mood. Oh, Zio Martinu, don't betray me if I confide things in you I wouldn't even tell my confessor.'

'If you thought that I would betray you, you

shouldn't have called me! I've heard of things like this before! Besides,' the old man then said, 'it doesn't matter if she doesn't have children, she'll lose her looks just the same.'

'Don't believe it, Zio Martinu! She's one of those women who'll get more beautiful in time, even if she isn't happy. There's no work in the house; if her husband treats her badly, the others – especially my mother – adore her. Anyway, I don't love her for her beauty! I love her because . . . she's who she is . . .'

'She'll grow old. You'll both grow old!'

'Ah, there's some time from now to then! What are you saying! You who are the wise one? You don't know what youth is? We'll end by falling into mortal sin, and then what?'

'But do you believe, Elias Portolu, that everything will be over if you become a priest? The man, the young man, won't die in you; you'll be able to fall just the same, and then it won't be a sin any longer, it'll be a sacrilege.'

'Oh, no! What are you saying?' said Elias with horror. 'Then it will be a different thing. She'll never look at me again; and I'll get them to send me to a village.'

'Fine, this is all fine, my son. But everything else aside, tell me. You're no longer a boy. Will they want you? To be a priest takes time, study, money; who knows if you can do it, who knows if you will be able to conquer temptation in the meanwhile!'

'Once I've announced my plan I won't worry; she won't look at me again, I'll conquer myself. I'm no

104

longer a boy, it's true, but I'm not yet thirty like that shepherd who sold his flock and became a priest in less than three years.'

'That is all fine; however, I'll tell you something else: I don't like men who become priests because of some disappointment, and especially some disappointment in love. It has to start when they're boys – they should do it because they have a vocation.'

'I have a vocation, and have had. I had it as a boy and then it returned when I was in *that place*. And, Zio Martinu, don't think that if I become a priest I do it out of laziness, or for money, or for living well, like so many others do. It's because I believe in God and want to conquer the temptations of the world.'

'That's not enough Elias Portolu. The man who becomes a priest must not only reject evil, but must do good. He must live only for others – he must, in other words, become a priest for others, and not for himself. Instead, you want to be a priest for yourself, to save your soul, not the soul of others. Think about it, Elias Portolu. Am I right or not?'

Elias became thoughtful. He felt that the wise old man was right, yes, but he didn't want to, couldn't, give up.

'So you advise me against it, Zio Martinu?' he said. 'But you should also think whether you are doing good or evil. Ask your conscience.'

Zio Martinu, who never lost his composure, seemed struck by Elias' last observation. His sharp eyes looked into the distance, towards the gauzy horizon, while his absorbed inner being heard mysterious voices vibrate in that great desert silence.

'My conscience would tell me to be angry with you, Elias Portolu,' he said after a moment of silence. 'Like your father said, you are not a man, you are a twig, a reed that bends at the first breath of wind. That's why you fall in love with a woman you cannot have, that you never wanted to have. That's why you want to be a bad priest, when you could be a useful man. You must be an eagle, not a thrush, Elias. Your father is right!'

And while Elias was weighed down by these harsh observations, the old man continued: 'Do you know what grief is, Elias Portolu? Ah, you think you have drunk all the bitterness of life because you were in prison and because you fell in love with your brother's wife? What is that? It's nothing. A man must spit on those little things. Grief is something else entirely, Elias, something else entirely. Have you felt the anguish of having to commit a crime? And then the remorse? And the misery. Do you know what misery is? And do you know what hate is? Or seeing your enemy, your rival triumph, become your master and then persecute you? Have you ever been betrayed? Betrayed by a woman, by a friend, by a relative? Have you cherished a dream for years and years and then seen it vanish in front of you like a cloud? Have you felt what it's like not to believe in anything, not to hope in anything, to see everything around you a void? Not believing in God, or believing Him unjust and hating Him because He has opened up ways for you and then closed them one by one, do you know what that means, Elias Portolu, do you know?'

'Zio Martinu, you frighten me,' Elias murmured.

'See what a man you are! You are frightened by only hearing talk about man's grief. Go, get up and go, Elias Portolu. Go! Go! Go! You are young, you are healthy, go and look life in the face. Be an eagle, not a thrush. Besides the Lord is great, often reserving joys for us we couldn't even imagine. Man must never despair. Who knows if in a year you won't be happy and laughing about your past? Go.'

Elias stood up.

The old man said: 'Eh, you are leaving me alone? You aren't taking me to the hut; not going to give me some junket and milk?'

'Come on, Zio Martinu. I'm as dazed as a foolish sheep.'

They walked along in silence. In the hut Elias gave the old man some milk, wine, bread and grapes, and they talked again of unimportant things. Before leaving, Zio Martinu suddenly turned back to the topic under discussion.

'Besides, there is always time. After you have really learned what life is, if you want to go into seclusion, do it. But remember what I've told you: better to be a man in the world doing good, than a man of the Lord come to evil. *Addio*, take care of yourself.'

Elias was left saddened, but calm; he even felt strong, and ashamed of his past weakness.

'The old boar is right. We have to be men,' he was thinking, 'we must be eagles, not thrushes. I want to

107

be strong. A good Christian, yes, but strong.' And for a few days he felt sad, but not desperate, and did everything to rid his mind of melancholy thoughts.

The autumn was extraordinarily mild and sweet in the *tanca*. The sky was serene, assuming that tender, inexpressible sweetness of a Sardinian autumn sky. On the faraway horizons and milky backgrounds the sky was like the sea; on some evenings the horizon became all milky pink like mother-of-pearl, with clouds of a pale blue that were like sails. Against the clarity of the sky the woods were outlined with a dark, damp tint. The leaves fell only from the bushes, but some oaks, lost in the vastness of the *tanca*, began to turn golden. And the tender thick grass grew, covering the brown stubble; some wild flowers, especially those near water, opened their melancholy violet petals.

The sun spread welcome warmth into every nook – on the bushes, on the walls, on the rocks; and in that sweetness of the sun under the tender sky, with its meadows of short, fine grass, the *tanca* seemed more vast, unlimited, with its borders lost on the shores of the placid seas on the horizon.

During that season life in the sheepfold went along calmly and was not fatiguing.

Zio Portolu was often absent, and Mattia led a somewhat wild and taciturn life. Mattia loved the flock, the dogs, the horse very much. The cat and the kid that had become a goat always followed him around, and he talked with them as with friends. For some time he had been very busy making hives of cork, wanting to make a beehive the following spring. He had simple tastes and no vices, but he was superstitious and a little fearful. He believed in dead and wandering spirits, and during the long nights in the *tanca* watching the sheep he had more than once grown pale seeming to see mysterious flashes in the air, strange animals running by without making a sound, and in that immense solitude of brush and rocks he often heard a faraway voice in the woods, mysterious laments, sighs, whispering.

Elias was a little envious of the character and simplicity of his brother.

'He is always as even tempered as a seven-year-old boy,' he thought. 'What does he think about? What does he want? He has never suffered and perhaps never will. He is not strong, but he is stronger than I am.'

At the end of that autumn, however, after the talk with Zio Martinu, he seemed finally to have acquired a certain energy; if nothing more he succeeded in controlling himself and making good plans for the future. But one day, going back to town, he found Pietro and Maddalena in a tempest. It was wheat-sowing time for Pietro, the seeds having been kept in an antique Sardinian ark of dark wood in the couple's bedroom. Now Pietro felt that a certain amount of these seeds were missing, and he had begun to mutter against his wife.

'What do you think I made with them?' Maddalena said, very offended. 'Bread or sweets? You know that there are no secrets in your house, and your mother here sees my every move.'

109

'She is right, my son,' Zia Annedda confirmed. 'You couldn't be missing any wheat. What would we do with it?'

'You women know! You make and tear apart, you have secret needs, foolishness, and to satisfy your whims you go to the provisions and use them up and deceive your poor husbands who work all year for you.'

Pietro spoke in the plural, but Maddalena knew that every word was meant for her.

'Speak to me,' she said, enraged. 'Don't talk to your mother. The wheat was in our room.'

'And it is missing from there.'

'You mean that I took it?'

'Yes,' yelled Pietro.

'Filthy!'

'Filthy – who? Me? Look here, daughter of Arrita Scada! Damn the day I married you!'

That and other insults. At this point Elias came in, and Zia Annedda went out to the courtyard to help him unload the saddlebag from the horse. Elias heard the quarrel and felt a pain in his heart.

'What's wrong with them?' he asked through clenched teeth. 'What has got into them? Ah!' he said out loud, after his mother spoke to him quietly. 'It's a disgrace. Is Pietro going crazy? Our house is becoming a scandal! It's time to stop this!'

'We've just begun!' said Pietro coming to the door with his eyes blazing with anger. 'And you keep your nose out of it, if you don't want to be part of it.'

'Man!' shouted Elias, 'watch what you're saying.'

'You watch out. I'm a man; but you're a nobody,

110

and don't stick your nose into my business.'

'Stop it, my sons, stop it. What is this? This has never happened in my house!' said Zia Annedda, mournful and deathly pale.

'I'm the boss,' Pietro said arrogantly, 'you have to listen to me. I'm the boss, and if someone wants to take over, I'm ready to squash him like a grasshopper.'

They went into the kitchen and Maddalena, after seeing Elias and hearing the words of Pietro and Zia Annedda, began to cry. This provoked Elias against Pietro, and Pietro against Maddalena.

'Of course, I need cry babies. Women, women! I need some cooperation, otherwise from now on there are people who will get acquainted with a club.'

'Just try it, coward!' Maddalena shouted, rising up threateningly. 'Mean devil, liar, coward . . .'

Pietro grew red with anger and threw himself on her shouting: 'Say that again, say that again, if you dare . . .'

'You're drunk . . .'

'Stop it!' Elias and Zia Annedda shouted together, causing him to stop.

Maddalena was sobbing and repeating: 'Liar, mean, mean, mean . . .'

'Now I'll make you see how drunk or mean I am!' yelled Pietro breaking loose; and he ran over and slapped her.

Elias turned livid and he felt himself trembling. Fortunately Zia Annedda stopped him, and Pietro still had enough good sense to go away, otherwise there could have been a disaster.

111

'This is just the beginning,' Pietro shouted from the courtyard in an angry, yet ironical, voice. 'You could have married that jewel, my brother! Now I'm going to get drunk and when I return, if anyone wants to lift as much as a finger, we'll see who's the lion and who's the lizard.'

And he left. Maddalena had stopped crying as soon as he slapped her; she was as white as a ghost and was trembling all over with anger and pain, but she had instantly understood that if she didn't change her ways it would cause serious trouble in the family.

'It's my fault,' she said in a trembling voice. 'Excuse me, it won't happen again; now that I have taken up my cross, I will know how to bear it. Pardon me, pardon me for the shame, pardon my tongue. Ah!' she then said while Elias, pale and silent, devoured her with his eyes, and Zia Annedda went to close the outside door, 'may my mother and brother and sister never learn of this!'

'She's a saint!' Elias was thinking. 'Ah, he doesn't deserve it; he's a ferocious beast!'

'You should have married her!' These words of Pietro's resounded in his mind, in his heart, in his throbbing blood.

'What if I had! What if I had! What a terrible mistake! Now they're unhappy because she doesn't love him, and he must be angry because of that, and I . . . what am I? I'm unhappier than either of them, and I love her more than before, and I . . .'

He felt the impetuous desire to take Maddalena in his arms and carry her away. It was time, it was time!

Who was keeping them apart? What was keeping them apart?

But Zia Annedda came back in and he returned to reality.

During the evening, however, he had the opportunity to be alone with Maddalena; she was silently working, sitting next to the open door, deep sighs rose from her heart from time to time, and her eyelids were violet. Elias went out, returned, he couldn't make up his mind to leave. A fatal fascination drew him to that open door, forcing him to circle around that young woman like a moth around a flame. Perhaps he thought Maddalena was more exhausted than she was, and he was more worn out with her grief than with his. Vain regrets, useless remorse, anger against Pietro, fatal desires were making him dizzy; at that moment of passion he would have given his life to comfort Maddalena, but he was unable to say a word to her, and he was secretly angry with his timidity.

'Aren't you going?' entreated Zia Annedda. 'Leave, my son, go while there is time. Go, they are waiting for you, go.'

'I'll go!' he answered finally, annoyed.

'Ah, my son, do you want to stir up trouble! Go, go. Your brother will come back drunk; you'll both make more trouble. Ah, my sons, you don't fear God, and temptation will make fools of you!'

Maddalena sighed almost groaning, and Elias was struck by his mother's words. It was true; the devil was tempting him, and he was waiting with bitter desire for his brother to come back so he could insult him to

113

make up for Maddalena's pain and humiliation. And that wasn't all; he was already looking at Maddalena differently from the way he had looked at her up to now. He was conscious of it all and felt a rush of terror.

'I am about to be lost, about to ruin us both!' he thought. 'What is my sacrifice worth? I gave up my brother's wife in order not to make him unhappy, and now it is I who want to make him miserable. Is it possible I am capable of so much? I?' he asked himself then with surprise. He seemed to have become a thief and the change surprised and frightened him. 'I must go and never come back,' he thought in the end.

He made up his mind and left, to the relief of his mother who was waiting for the moment with trepidation. Maddalena kept her place and didn't even raise her large violet eyelids of the Madonna; but on leaving he gave her a desperate look and went away with death in his heart.

A deep, tragic sorrow gripped him from that day. He began to despair of himself and everything, and to hate his fellow man. Up to that time his desperation and need for solitude had been something sweet and good; now they became bad, bitter, accompanied as they were by an instinctive desire for revenge. Elias Portolu felt that fate, the wicked sphinx that tormented men, had been unjust to him. He had tried to do good, sacrificing himself, and instead of good it had changed into evil for him. Why? What destiny had the right to play with men? In the immense solitude of the *tanca*, under the pale autumn sky, in the mysterious sorrow of the deserted landscape with the hazy horizons, the

114

shepherd's soul asked the terrible questions of learned men, but without being able to give himself an explanation. Only sorrow remained, and in the sorrow he lost not only his faith, but he began to stir up the monster of rebellion.

More than once, wandering through the confines of the *tanca*, Elias saw that old pagan Zio Martinu, whose rigid shape dominated and at the same time formed a thing itself in the strong, sad, fatal landscape. But he always irritably disappeared.

'He is an old beast,' he thought. 'What is pain? What is sorrow? The old man of stone laughed at me, but with all his sins and all his misfortune and his wisdom he doesn't know that I suffer more in a day than he has his whole life. He'd better not come around with his sermons any more or I'll kill him with an axe.'

And yet he felt that the old man wouldn't harm him; indeed, the opposite, if only he had followed his advice! . . . But he was angry with everyone, and most of all with himself, and he felt a cruel need to hurt someone, as though he were a child, to feel not pleasure, but pain.

In fact, a little boy would come to the sheepfold, the son of a shepherd neighbour, very poor people. He was a little silly but good, ragged, so thin and dark that he seemed like a bronze statuette. Almost every day he came to the Portolus' hut and played quietly with the cat, the piglet and the dogs. Elias often gave him bread, fruit and milk, and even wine; and the little boy was fond of him. But one day cancelled out all the others. Elias was alone in the hut and in a terrible mood because the evening before Mattia had brought bad news from home. Pietro was drunk every time he came home from work and insulted and mistreated Maddalena. The boy came up quietly in his bare feet, embraced the dog and then entered the hut.

'What do you want?' Elias asked crossly.

'I want some milk!'

'We don't have any.'

'I want some milk, I want some, I want some,' the little boy kept repeating.

Elias felt an uncontrollable anger. He took the little one by the arm and threw him out with a kick, insulting him like an adult and ordering him never to come back. The boy went away almost with dignity, without saying a word; but after a few minutes Elias heard him crying in the distance; a desolate, desperate cry that echoed sadly in the solitude; and he felt a surge of anger against himself, a violent urge to bite his fists until they bled. That cry seemed like the echo of his own sorrow. An infinite desperation enveloped him.

'I'm an animal, I'm lost. But are the others any different from me? We're all evil; with the difference that the others don't have scruples and are happy, while I suffer because I've been a fool, because I did right by someone who didn't deserve it.'

Memories of *that place* also rose up in him insistently, from the depths of his soul; and it seemed to him that the pain caused by that sentence had been nothing in

116

comparison to the pain he now felt. However, in the meantime the memory of past pain increased that of the present; forgotten details returned to his mind with bitterness; memories of the humiliations, the extortions, the persecutions of the *aguzzini*, as he called the prison guards, made him grow red with anger. Ah, if only he had one of them in his hands at this very moment in the solitary *tanca*! . . .

'I would cut him to pieces,' he thought, grinding his teeth, 'and then I would lick the blood off my knife.'

In short, it seemed that a ferocious beast thrashed around in that pale young man with the mild appearance who was often seen sitting near the hut, with his elbows on his knees, immersed in his little holy books.

In the meantime the cold came, the immense sadness of winter in its solitude; and Elias' weak constitution felt it profoundly. It is in winter that the Sardinian shepherd works and suffers the most. And so the long days of rain, snow, overwork, discomfort of the hut always full of smoke and wind, the struggle against the elements, finally exhausted the physical and moral strength of Elias.

At this time, during certain snowfalls that froze the sheep to death, the idea of becoming a priest returned to the young man. But how different from before! In the harsh struggle with the elements and with himself he despaired more than ever, he felt a rebellious desire for a comfortable life, for a truce, and he saw a change of condition as his only possibility of escape.

And at the same time an evil fascination often drew

117

him to town, to the warm little house where Maddalena worked next to the fire. A relative peace now reigned between the couple. At least Maddalena had become prudent, and sometimes only Pietro's drunken voice was heard. But whether or not she was happy, Elias wasn't able to tell. The bad seed had germinated; day by day one more drop brought the vase to brimming and was about to overflow. Elias abandoned himself secretly and entirely to his passion. He was thinking: 'No one will know, much less her; but who can keep me from looking at her? What wrong am I doing? That's the only happiness I have. Don't I have the right to a little happiness?'

He saw her often, and watched her, and instinctively wanted her to notice he was looking at her; and too often she noticed and unconsciously responded to his looks. And when their looks met, a shiver, a suspension of life, a vertigo of sad pleasure took him out of himself.

They were close to losing themselves. Only the opportunity was missing. At the end of winter Elias was taken by a real frenzy of love; he could reason no more; and along with the atrocious suffering he felt a sad happiness in feeling himself loved again by Maddalena. Everything that before seemed wrong and painful now seemed right, happy; everything that awakened horror before now dizzily attracted him.

On the last day of the carnival he, Pietro, Maddalena and two other young women put on masks. The couple was on good terms, indeed Pietro was happy beyond words. Zia Annedda weakly opposed the plan of that masquerade, but they paid

118

no attention to her. With her simple good sense she disapproved of masquerades, dances, carnival activities; and she made Maddalena promise at least not to dance, especially with other masqueraders she didn't know, and especially the dances from the continent, those that allowed the couples to hold and touch each other.

Maddalena and her women friends dressed as cats, that is, putting on two long dark skirts, one tied at the waist, the other at the neck, and their heads wrapped up in a shawl; the men masqueraded as Turks,[12] with large white cassocks tight at their ankles, and feminine bodices of bright-coloured brocade, reversed, tied behind with the back part in front.

They left at an hour when the road was deserted and went down streets where Nuoro assumes the aspect of a little city. The women went along a little timidly, attempting to change their walk, afraid of being recognized, their laughter of childish joy smothered under the wax masks.

The men went roughly ahead, as though to clear the way for their companions. From time to time Pietro gave out a wild, gutteral cry, stretching his neck like a rooster. Then Elias remembered the riders' cries of joy on their way to St Francis' church on one pure May morning. His heart had been pounding from the first moment that he, having learned a little about continental dancing from *that place*, had said to himself: 'I'll dance with Maddalena.'

Never mind Zia Annedda's prohibition or Maddalena's promise. He was burning with the desire

119

to dance with her, and he would have gone through any obstacle whatever to achieve his aim.

A wild and rebel strength stirred within him. As once he had succeeded in controlling himself and in wanting good for others, now he felt all the audacity of evil and wanted to satisfy his worst instincts. He felt his face burning under his mask, and the tight and irksome costume made his arms and legs hot. Besides, the day was warm, overcast, and in the sweet air he already felt the promise of spring.

The streets were crowded; simple and fancy masqueraders were walking up and down, among the noisy cloud of dirty little urchins shouting insults and indecent words. Wearing only masks, or with brightly coloured clothes, people were passing, followed by the enquiring and scoffing looks of the workers and bourgeois. Women, little girls, servants with blood-red bodices went by. Groups of drunken townsmen pushed one another on the Corso; and the melancholy music of guitar and accordion rose and vibrated in that warm and hazy air that made the sounds more distinct, as in an autumn twilight.

It was enough to daze Elias, used to the great solitude of the *tanca*. In vain he had thought he had known the world and been ready for anything because he had crossed the sea and seen the sad multitude in *that place*. Ah, now that little carnival at Nuoro was enough, the multicoloured crowd, that melancholy quadrille wept by a wandering accordion, to make him feel lost in that world not his, and everything seemed different to him. It seemed to him that all the

120

people that were walking, talking, laughing were happy, even drunk with happiness, and he also abandoned himself without scruple to the folly of his desires, to an irresistible need for joy and pleasure.

Now Pietro and he were walking with their companions, protecting them against the blows and tricks of the ruffians. Maddalena walked in the middle, but every once in a while pushed ahead and looked now at her husband, now at Elias, who always replied to that look with burning and oblique eyes under the mask.

'Let's do something, let's stop. Going back and forth like this is stupid,' Elias said to his companion.

'As you wish,' she answered and communicated the young man's request to Maddalena.

'What should we do?' Maddalena asked.

'Dance. Look, they're dancing over there, let's join in.'

'Your brother wants to dance,' Maddalena said to Pietro.

'No.'

'Yes.' The women said.

'My mother doesn't want us to.'

'Let's dance. The Sardinian dance.'

And the three women skipped ahead gaily, running toward the place where they were dancing to the accordion music. A circle of townspeople, little urchins, workers, almost all pale, ugly, insolent faces, surrounded some of the masked couples who were dancing, bumping into each other and laughing.

A man dressed like a woman, with a red, bearded face, wearing his mask backwards, was playing the accordion with great seriousness, his eyes fixed on the keys. It was a polka played well enough, but sad and melancholy like barrel-organ music.

The masqueraders broke the circle of the curious bystanders and entered the dance area, while other breathless couples stopped, tired but not ready to quit entirely. No one complained about the newcomers; indeed, a man dressed as a monk, with his face painted yellow, immediately invited one of the young women to dance and she accepted without much urging. Elias found himself next to Maddalena; he was trembling with desire to dance, but now, just at that moment, he didn't dare for fear of Pietro.

'Play the Sardinian dance,' Pietro shouted to the musician. The musician looked up, stared at the Turk for a moment, but didn't stop.

'Quiet!' shouted the couples dancing past Pietro.

'All right, then. Quiet!' he said as though to himself, deeply embarrassed.

'Come on now, you dance too!' said the masked woman dancing with the monk, passing in front of her companions.

'Yes, let's dance, let's dance; why are we standing here like this?' begged the other masquerader, turning to Pietro.

He looked her in the eyes, opened his arms and said: 'Good, let's dance, otherwise you'll die from desire; but watch out because I don't know how to dance, and if I step on your toes it will be your fault.'

He took her in his arms and began to jump and gyrate in a comic way with her. Fortunately one of the masqueraders, with a long cape of coarse wool tied round his waist with a rope, came to liberate the young woman, pleading with Pietro to give her to him. Then he stepped back, stopped, and saw that Elias and Maddalena were dancing together.

'Eh, they know how to dance!' he said to himself good-naturedly. 'If Zia Annedda could see them, she would truly beat them!'

Elias and Maddalena danced well, composed. But they weren't paying much attention to the dance, after finding themselves in each other's arms almost without realizing it, dazed by a nameless intoxication. Elias felt his heart beating wildly, and Maddalena saw that circle of pale, ugly, insolent faces wheeling dizzily around her.

'I'd like to talk to her, but what can I say?' Elias asked himself, holding the back of the skirt that fell from her collar with a desperate grip. But in vain he anxiously searched for a word, just one word to say to her. He only felt an insane urge to pick her up in his arms, break through the circle of the foolish curious, fly far away into the solitude, howling his pain and passion in one great cry. But Pietro was there, standing still, terrible as a sphinx under his grotesquely laughing mask, and for some time Elias had a strange fear of his brother.

Did Pietro know? Did he guess? Was it possible he was so stupid as not to read in his brother's eyes the cruel passion devouring him?

'Why should I care?' Elias thought after frightening

himself with those questions. 'Let him see and kill me if he likes; I would be glad.'

He felt no grudge against Pietro; he only had fear and often a strange, childish compassion for his brother.

'He is worse off than I because he loves his wife and she doesn't love him,' he thought. 'Pietro, my brother, what a wrong we have done!'

While he was dancing, overwhelmed by the impulse of his insane desires, his mind went over all these confused thoughts; and he felt passion, pity, fear, sorrow and pleasure at the same time. The sound of the accordion, the noise of the crowd, that phantasmagoria of faces and colours, the movement, the masks, the contact with Maddalena dazed him and burned in his blood. There was a moment when he could no longer see. Panting, he bent over and said something to Maddalena that she did not understand, but that made her raise her eyes to him. He looked at her long, desperately; and from that moment he had only one fixed, devouring thought.

The dance ended; the circle of curious disbanded, and our masqueraders began wandering through the streets again among the crowd. The evening fell, pale and hazy. And following his companions as in a dream, Elias found himself in the lane in front of his silent little house, facing the still hedge in the twilight. The quiet cat in the window, with its eyes fixed on the distance, seemed immersed in contemplation of the grey and violet mountains looming on the horizon. A fire was burning in the *focolare*.

Zia Annedda was waiting in the courtyard with her hands crossed under her apron. She was praying against the temptation that could overcome her masked sons (for her a mask was a symbol of the devil), and at the eruption of the group she started slightly. Perhaps an inner evil spirit had whispered to her that her prayer was useless, that the devil would win, that with the return of her masked sons mortal sin would enter the little house pure till then.

'Did you have a good time? It was time to come back!' she complained.

'We're late,' agreed Maddalena, but without regret. 'Come, come, I'm dying from the heat.'

And she preceded her companions up the outer stairway. Elias took off his mask, and Pietro, who had already removed his before entering, ran to the pitcher of water and drank deeply.

'What a thirst you have,' said Zia Annedda.

'Thirst and hunger, mama; give me something to eat, then I'm going to the *seranu*.'

And Pietro went to the table against the wall where there was a basket of bread and some leftovers. (That day the Portolus had had a sumptuous dinner: boiled beans with lard, and *cattas*.)

'You're crazy,' said Zia Annedda. 'May St Francis bless you; what are you thinking of doing? You'll have supper with us, then you'll go to sleep. These aren't nights to go out. Go and change your clothes.'

'Why, no, certainly not, *mamma mia*! The carnival comes only once a year! I'm going to dance and my

125

brother Elias will come too. It's been a year since we were all together!'

Elias, all flushed and goodlooking in his woman's disguise, turned sullen. Did his brother's words cause him pain? Or was he ashamed of the surge of joy that Pietro's plans to spend the night out had given him?

'You're mistaken if you think I want to go dancing,' Elias said; then he plucked up courage and added: 'It'd be better if you didn't go either.'

'You hear, Pietro?'

'No, I'm going back. Look, I'll eat now, then I'll go. And you'll come, too, Elias; you'll see what fun it'll be. Come and eat.'

'No, no, in fact I'm going to get changed.'

'Give me some wine, mamma. Ah, if you only knew how much fun we had! We have . . . no, we haven't danced, don't believe it even if they tell you!' exclaimed Pietro, eating large mouthfuls. 'Ha, youth is the time for enjoyment. And then what harm is it? And even if I don't know how to dance I had fun just the same. Eh, those women, how they enjoy themselves. Oh, that monk! And that great coat? Ha, ha!' he said as though laughing to himself.

'Well, then, at least take care not to dirty the bodice; may St Francis bless you! Do you want some cheese? Ah, temptation is carrying you away, my boys; but after this comes Lent. Will you at least go to confession?'

Elias started. For some seconds he stood still in the doorway, undecided, as though concentrating on another distant voice.

126

'You should eat with Pietro and go out afterwards with him,' this voice said to him. 'Do you hear your mother? Will you go to confession?'

But he was unable, he was not able to pay attention to this voice. Ah, temptation overcame him, gripped him; it was a thousand times stronger than he. Useless to fight because it had already won, and had for some time. He went in and changed; then he sat in the courtyard in the place where his mother had been earlier, and he was gripped by a single desire; that Pietro go away; and by a single fear; that Pietro might stay at home. But a little after Maddalena's girlfriends went away, Pietro came out into the courtyard and said to his brother: 'You're not coming, then?'

'No.'

'You're an idiot. I'm going to enjoy myself. Will you open the door for me later?'

Elias did not answer. All bent over, with his elbows on his knees and his head in his hands, he shook with pain and pleasure and did not dare to look at his brother again. And Pietro went away.

'Come to supper,' Zia Annedda said two times from the doorway.

'I'm not hungry; I don't feel well,' answered Elias; and he remained still for a long hour, always in the same position, with his head in his hands.

Inside he heard Maddalena chattering happily, as he had never heard her, in a different voice; she was telling Zia Annedda all the details of the masquerade, and was laughing, and her eyes must be shining, her face lit up, her spirit inebriated. Then the two women

127

retired and everything was silent around Elias. The fire still burned in the *focolare*; a fearful quiet was in the air, in the tranquil courtyard, in the hazy night.

He got up; his back was broken, his heart pounding; his blood surged through his back, his neck, and bounded to his head, clouding his thoughts. In this unconscious state he went up the ladder without making a sound and knocked lightly on Maddalena's door. She must have been awake because she said immediately: 'Who is it?'

'Open the door,' he said in a low voice. 'It's me; I have to tell you something.'

'Wait a minute,' she answered calmly. Presently she opened the door. 'What do you want? Are you feeling ill, Elias? What's the matter.'

As she said this she looked at him and grew pale. Perhaps she had opened the door innocently, but now, seeing him so white-faced, with eyes like a madman, she understood everything and was shaken.

He went in and closed the door. And she – who could have shouted and saved herself – was silent and made no move.

VII

Pietro came back very late, dead drunk. Elias opened the door for him and then went back to bed; but he was in the courtyard again before daylight, and it was barely dawn when he left for the sheepfold.

It was a sad, grey dawn, but not cold. The sky was covered with one great foggy, unmoving cloud that weighed on the dead landscape like a grey stone vault. Elias rode alone, lost in that deadly silence. Not a voice was heard, not a leaf moved. Even the rivulets along the edge of the paths ran by green, cold, silent. Elias' face was the colour of that grey sky, and the shadows around his eyes were as green, cold and sad as the water.

He seemed to be just waking up from a wonderful and at the same time a horrible dream; a monster of happiness and anguish ransacked his heart. The happiness, however – if happiness it could be called –

129

was never separate from a sense of anguish, and when the pain of the committed sin overcame him (which was most of the time), nothing could ease it.

The good and faithful part of Elias' soul awoke suddenly on that sad and menacing Lenten dawn, and he was distressed and appalled before the reality of the thing done.

'It's not true, it was a dream,' he thought, squeezing the reins in his fingers stiff with terror. 'A dream. Oh, what I dreamed about on the banks of the Isalle and in the *tanca* so many times! But no, no, no! What are you saying Elias Portolu? Wretched man, you're crazy, the most vile, the most abject of men.'

But while he went on reviling himself memories returned and his whole body started with pleasure and his face became serene; then he became more disturbed than before. A wave of shame and remorse entered every vein; and again the terror and wild impulse to beat himself, to bite his fists, attacked him like rabid dogs.

The abuse began all over again.

'You are a vile, wretched madman, gaolbird Elias Portolu. What can your mother, your father, your brothers expect from you? You have stained your own house, you have betrayed your brother, your mother, your own self. Cain, Judas, vile, foul, filthy beggar. What will you do now; what is left for you to do now, except to kill yourself?'

His memories flooded back and he felt that now he would love Maddalena until he died, and at the first opportunity he would fall again; and his hair stood on

130

end with horror at this thought. And so the journey went. Going beyond the edge of the *tanca* he slowly raised his eyes and, as though dreaming, looked at the landscape stretched out before him, silent and green, a sad wintry green. The rocks, the edge of the woods, grave and still against a grey sky all seemed changed, everything was against him.

'What have I done? What have I done? How can I bear my father looking at me?'

And yet he not only bore it, but he had to listen to the cruelly wounding words of Zio Portolu.

'Did you have a good time, my lamb? Ha, I can see it in your face. Your face is the colour of yeast; you wore a mask and danced and stayed up late and enjoyed yourself. I can see it in your eyes, my son. Your father was here working, keeping an eye on thieves while you enjoyed yourself. Come on. Ha, don't think I'm envious; it's your time. Mine has passed, and now it's Lent. What is Zia Annedda doing? Ah, she has sent me some *focacce* and *frittelle*. Ah, she didn't forget the old shepherd. And what is my Maddalennedda doing? Is she having a good time? Yes, let's let her have a good time, the little dove. She's a saint like Zia Annedda; eh, she resembles her more than her own sons.'

'If he only knew,' Elias was thinking with a shudder. Each of his father's words struck his heart. He couldn't be left to his own thoughts in the presence of Zio Portolu, so as soon as he could he went in search of solitude; and, without admitting it to himself, he wanted to meet up with Zio Martinu. But the old man was not there. Crossing the *tanca* Elias only met his brother Mattia who, calm and taciturn, was wandering around armed with a long pole. No one else. Under that great dead sky, in the total stillness, the *tancas* seemed even more deserted and boundless.

Elias thought again about the masquerade, the sounds and colours of the crowd, dancing with Maddalena; and each small remembrance made him shudder. Ah, everyone he had seen was happy, and only he was condemned to wander in solitude, and to have his happiness change into torment. He began to rebel: and anyway, since the first step was taken, since his soul was inexorably lost, why not continue enjoying himself?

'I'm an idiot,' he thought. 'Maddalena cannot live without me, she's told me that, and I swore I would always be hers. Why should I make her unhappy? We won't do any more evil in the world; we'll live together as husband and wife, and Pietro will never suffer by our sin.' And his face was serene with the dream of such happiness; but suddenly he felt the horror of his dream and wanted to roll on the ground, unearth rocks, shout his sin to heaven, hit his head against the stones to forget, to remove the memories and desires from his mind.

By dusk he was overcome by a sadness and unconquerable languor. He began to look at the horizon toward Nuoro with the desire to return, to see Maddalena; at least to see her from a distance, at least to squeeze her hand, at least to lean his head on her apron and cry like a baby.

132

'I'll go, I'll go,' he murmured, like that night when fever had felled him under a tree. 'I'll go, I'll go.'

And there was a moment when he started on his way; but at the first step he realized that not only his desire to see Maddalena was pushing him, but also mortal sin, the devil, the monster of the fallen.

'Where are you going, Elias Portolu? Is it possible you are not a man?' And he didn't go; but he was afraid of himself and of his weakness; and the thought occurred to him to throw himself at his father's feet and confess everything and to beg: 'Tie me up, father, keep me here; don't let me go, don't leave me alone, help me fight the devil.'

'Oh, God, he'd kill me if I said that to him!' was his next thought. 'And he'd be right to crush me under his foot, like a frog.'

For several days he struggled like this; after the victory of the first evening, the following days were less terrible, and he did not go back to Nuoro. But his strength left him, a mortal sadness gave him rest neither day nor night. He felt that he could no longer resist temptation if he went back to town and saw Maddalena again.

Then he went looking for Zio Martinu again. He crossed the *tanca*, jumped over the wall and went into the woods. It was a very clear moonlit night; the wind passed high in the trees, causing a continuous, sonorous rustling; but inside the woods under the cork trees not a leaf moved. The clear, calm moon passed through the branches; in the silver background other woods

133

appeared like black mountains. It was like a fairytale forest.

Elias kept walking. His sharp eyes distinguished the cracks in the ground, the trunks in the shade, every little shrub; from a distance he saw that the little hut of Zio Martinu was illuminated, and suddenly in the sadness that had driven him on, he felt relief.

Ah! Finally he would be able to tell someone the horrible secret that was crushing his heart, to ask help and advice; but arriving at the hut he greeted Zio Martinu and again fell into despair. What could that old man do for him, say to him? Fact was fact, and whatever happened, there was no remedy. And what had to happen would have happened all the same, whatever the old man's advice.

He remembered how many times Zio Martinu had given him good advice; he had always felt comforted, but he had never been able to follow it. Thinking about it, he sat down next to the fire with such a visible expression of pain on his face that Zio Martinu immediately guessed everything.

'Where have you been?' said Elias. 'I've looked for you many times.'

'Why were you looking for me, Elias Portolu?'

'I hadn't seen you for such a long time.'

'And now where are you going so late at night?'

'I came here, Zio Martinu.'

'Have you been to town?'

'No, not after the last day of carnival.'

'You looked for me after that?'

134

'Yes,' said Elias; then he felt Zio Martinu guessed everything and he blushed.

'You are haggard,' Zio Martinu said, looking at his face. 'You carry the sign of mortal sin in your face. Why look for me if you have no more need of advice?'

Like the other times Elias raised wide, frightened, lost eyes to the old man's boar eyes, wild and yet sweet at the same time. And Zio Martinu felt his stone heart move. It seemed to him that Elias Portolu, that boy as beautiful and weak as a woman, was seeking refuge in him like a little lamb under a cork tree during a storm.

'Why scold him?' he thought. 'He suffers, you can see that, he turns red; fighting with him is like striking a sword against a cane.' Nevertheless he asked in a rough voice: 'Why did you come here now, Elias Portolu? What do you want me to say? If only you had followed my earlier advice!'

'Words! Words!' Elias burst out in real desperation. 'How do we know that my brother wouldn't have killed me if I had followed your advice? And yet I wouldn't have offended him like I have done now; and now he won't hurt a hair on my head. The world is like that, Zio Martinu! And it's fate and the devil who persecute us.'

'So why have you come now?'

'All right, then, yes,' continued Elias, ever more desperate and irritated, 'yes, I've come to ask your advice again, and I know your advice will be good; and I've come to ask your help and I'm certain that, in order to keep me from going back to Nuoro until the

135

temptation has stopped tormenting me, you would be capable of tying me up, of hiding me. But how do I know if I can follow your advice, or if while you're tying me up I won't try to bite your hands and run to do what the devil wants?'

'The devil! The devil!' the old man said shrugging his shoulders in contempt. 'You keep talking about the devil! I'm fed up with hearing you talk like that. Who is the devil? We're the devil.'

'You don't believe in the devil? And God?'

'I don't believe in anything, Elias Portolu! But when I've asked for advice I have followed it, and when I've asked for help I've kissed the hand that gave it to me, not bitten it; may a viper bite you, Elias Portolu!'

Elias smiled sadly. 'It was just a manner of speaking, Zio Martinu.'

'Good. And in a manner of speaking I'll tell you that since you come to ask for advice in order not to follow it, and to ask me to tie you up so that you can bite my hand, it wasn't worth your trouble, Elias Portolu. You believe in the devil. Well, take it by the horns and tie it up, but be careful it doesn't bite you.'

The old man was mocking him, and the pungent sarcasm that the Orunesi know how to give their words spewed more from his tone than from what he said. A childish anguish spread over Elias' face.

'Zio Martinu,' he said pleadingly, 'is this all your wisdom, to kill a desperate man?'

'Elias Portolu, I am not a wise man, but I know that each man must wear the shoe that fits his foot. You,

136

who believe in God and the devil, have come to ask advice from me who believes only in the strength of man; you have erred, and I have erred also by giving you advice that was not suitable to your character. So much for my wisdom, Elias! Ah, a donkey is wiser than I am! Who knows if instead of helping you I've hurt you? You must go to a man of God and ask his advice. But you must hurry. That is what I say.'

Elias felt that the old man was right, and suddenly he remembered Father Porcheddu and a conversation they had had one moonlit night on the heights of St Francis.

'I know a man of God, in fact,' he said. 'Once he gave me good advice and made me strong against temptation. He is a happy man who enjoys himself, but deep down he's a man of conscience. And cunning! And just like you, Zio Martinu, he guessed my secret immediately, while no one else I live with every day had guessed it. I'll go to Father Porcheddu.'

'Is he from Nuoro?'

'He's not Nuorese, but he lives in Nuoro.'

'All right, go then. Go right away.'

'I'm afraid, Zio Martinu.'

'What are you afraid of, little rabbit?' shouted the old man.

'I'm afraid of finding myself alone with Maddalena,' replied Elias with bewildered eyes.

'Ah, Elias Portolu, you make me laugh! What kind of animal are you? Are you a rabbit? A cat? A chicken? A lizard?'

'I'm a mortal man!'

137

'All right, then,' shouted Zio Martinu, 'I'll come with you. I won't leave you alone. You've become such a nuisance I'll take you to hell, if you want, to get rid of you.'

This promise made Elias smile and it calmed him. At last he saw a gleam of light ahead. He was thinking, 'Yes, I'll go to confession, I'll go to communion, I'll save my soul.'

His sorrow and passion did not leave him for a single instant, and the thought of having to renounce Maddalena forever, now that she was all his, gave him an inexpressible heartache; but the first step away from sin was now taken, and the others seemed less difficult.

The next morning Zio Martinu came to get him, and they started off for Nuoro on foot. On the way they didn't exchange twenty words. During the night Elias had made his examination of conscience, and now walking along he repeated his sins and good intentions; but as he neared the town he felt oppressed by a deathly anxiety.

'Listen, Zio Martinu,' he said suddenly, 'let's not go home.'

'Ah, what man is this!' the old man exclaimed, as though talking to himself. 'He goes to confession for fear of himself, not for fear of God, and he never knows how to get hold of himself.'

'Oh, all right, let's go home!' Elias said, almost irritated.

Luckily Maddalena was out, but he realized how weak he was when he was saddened by not seeing her,

138

and he didn't dare ask where she was. Then he and the old man went to Father Porcheddu's and waited for him to return from the choir. Father Porcheddu was a beneficed singer and surely had no hope of becoming a canon; nevertheless he lived comfortably, lovingly served by his old sister Anna, in a little house still furnished in the custom of his native village, with high four-poster wooden beds and black wood chests and high-backed chairs with straw seats.

The villagers sent him large provisions of wine, nuts, onions, beans and dried fruit; and old Anna knew how to prepare every kind of preserves, sweets, *sapa*, and the most delicious coffee in Nuoro.

When she learned that the young man with the restless eyes looking for Father Porcheddu was the son of Zia Annedda Portolu, she welcomed him warmly. Ah, she knew that saintly little woman because once Zia Annedda had cured her injured hand without asking anything in return.

'For the souls, for the little souls of purgatory!' Zia Annedda would say to her patients.

Finally Father Porcheddu came back; he was always the same, ruddy and cheerful, and greeted Elias with exclamations of joy, while looking at him steadily and mischievously.

'He's guessed too!' thought the young man, and felt himself grow pale with shame.

'I must speak with you . . .' he murmured.

'And this old oak?' asked Father Porcheddu, turning toward Zio Martinu. 'Let's go, let's go upstairs.

139

Annessa, bring some coffee and something stronger, if you have it.'

'Now I'll go along,' said Zio Martinu. 'I'll wait for you at your house, Elias Portolu. Good day, Father; take care of this young man.' But Father Porcheddu wouldn't let him go until Zia Annessa had poured a glass of *aquavite*, and then another.

Then Zio Martinu returned to the Portolus' and sat waiting by the *focolare*. When Elias came back, Maddalena was still out, and he was sorry about it, but not as much as an hour before. No. Now he wanted to see her again to demonstrate to himself, and also a little to Zio Martinu, how strong he was; he would have looked at her without passion or desire, with pure and penitent eyes.

And something really was new, a pure and ardent flame now shone in his face, but he looked deathly pale and his hands trembled. Zio Martinu looked long at him, in silence, then he asked if they shouldn't leave right away. Elias overcame the desire to test his strength by seeing Maddalena again and left.

'I have confessed,' he said to the old man as soon as they were alone. 'I'll come back in two weeks to take communion, and because Father Porcheddu must give me an answer.'

'What answer?'

'I'm going to be a priest,' Elias said, lowering his voice. 'Oh, it's time! That's the road for me to take.'

The old man did not reply. There seemed once again a wide gulf between him and Elias, and he was no more concerned about the young man's affairs.

Elias, however, was not offended; he, too, felt detached from the old man and from everything of his past.

A kind of ecstasy enveloped him. All anguish, worry, shame, indecision had ceased; ahead he saw a smooth white road like the road they were walking on, and a clear, serene background like the blue horizon of that pure morning.

'Father Porcheddu has taken an interest, he'll do everything, and in two or three weeks everything will be ready,' he said in an emotional voice, talking more to himself than to Zio Martinu. 'And everything will turn out fine, you'll see. There'll be expenses, but my father has money and he'll help me.'

'All right, all right, if that is your road, take it once and for all,' said Zio Martinu.

They separated at the sheepfold, and Elias didn't even thank the man who had led him to salvation; he only said: 'Let us see you once in a while, Zio Martinu.'

The old man promised nothing and didn't let himself be seen. A month later Elias noticed him at a distance, but avoided him.

'Oh, oh,' Zio Martinu thought with a strange smile in his little boar's eyes, 'if he's on his way to becoming a man of God, he really has a good start!'

What happened to Elias? A month went by, Lent ended, and Father Porcheddu was still waiting in vain. For the first days after his confession the young man had lived between heaven and earth; all his past was forgotten; all his future appeared sweet. He felt reborn with the pureness and sweetness of nature that was renewed around him in that beginning of spring. He prayed continually and waited with a sweet anxiety for the two weeks to pass. His face was serene; his eyes had a childlike transparency and expression.

But fifteen days of waiting were too much. Ah, Father Porcheddu must not know the human heart as well as he boasts, if he could believe that the joy of confession could last two weeks in a heart ravished by passion. Time passed, throwing a veil over Elias' joy; a day arrived during the second week when he felt plunged again into sadness; it was as though the hand of an invisible monster had taken him by the nape of the neck and pushed him towards an abyss.

The next day Elias thought again of returning to town, of throwing himself at Father Porcheddu's feet; but if he saw Maddalena first? A shiver ran through him at this question. Ah, it was useless, useless. He would always love Maddalena and never be able to forget her. At the moment when he believed he had conquered, had buried, his heart, feelings, the past, his passion got a more tenacious hold on him and swept him away like a leaf in a whirlwind. And the hand of that invisible monster that had him by the neck continued to push him towards sin. His face turned livid, his eyes gloomy.

One day when he was by chance standing near the opening of the *tanca*, thoughtful and sad, he saw an extraordinary thing. That morning, as usual, Mattia had gone to Nuro; he was to come back around noon, and now the warm noontime of March was enthroned in the *tanca*. It was a sweet hour of sun, of dreams. Not a human voice was heard, not a live soul was seen in the vastness of the plain. The warm wind bent the sun-warmed grass.

And here instead of Mattia, Elias saw Maddalena arriving on the horse with the white streak on its hoof, still followed by the now big colt. Was it an hallucination? A dream of his sick mind? Maddalena had never come to the sheepfold alone. Elias looked pale, troubled. It was she, it was she. There were those burning eyes fixed on his, even from a distance, with a magnetic power.

Not even for an instant did he have the desire or the strength to go away. He just let himself fall in a sitting position on the wall. Maddalena came without haste, but as soon as she reached the opening she dismounted with agility and came toward Elias. She was trembling all over and looked at him with wild passion. Ah, what expression and what light had those dark, burning, half-closed eyes! He never forgot them, and at that moment felt that that look gave him more joy in one mere instant than would an eternity of the joy felt the week before.

'And Mattia?' he asked.

'He stayed in town; I persuaded him to let me come. Pietro is not there, your mother has gone to gather olives and won't return until dusk.'

'Maddalena, you'll ruin us! Why have you come?'

She bent over him in a delirium.

'And why haven't you come back? Why haven't you, Elias? Elias! Elias!' she continued to moan in his face, taking his face in her hands with growing

143

agitation. 'Don't you see that I'm dying? Since you won't come, I've come here!' And she covered his face with kisses. He could no longer see and jumped up delirious with the same madness. And they were lost again.

Father Porcheddu waited for Elias in vain all during Lent; he asked about him, and when he learned that the young man often returned to town he became suspicious.

'He must have fallen again!' he thought. 'And I'll make a great impression on the monsignor now that the negotiations for him to enter the seminary have turned out well. Priest! Priest! He certainly wants to become a priest! And yet something must be done or otherwise a tragedy might take place in that house!' Then he went around looking for Elias himself until he found him.

'I've been waiting for you,' he said, looking him in the eye. But Elias' cold and wicked eyes avoided the look of the man of God. And his face was haggard, burned by passion and sin.

'I couldn't come.'

'Why couldn't you?'

'I thought it over; I'm unworthy to take communion, and besides, my mind isn't made up. There's still time, Father Porcheddu!'

'There's time, Elias? What are you saying, Elias! Woe to him who waits for tomorrow! You've fallen back into sin, the devil has you.'

144

'No, I'm not in sin! What did you come to tell me,' Elias said indifferently.

Father Porcheddu was appalled; he would have preferred for Elias to confess his sin, even rebelling, even cursing; but that coldness, that dissimulation was the height of perdition.

'Elias! Elias!' he said in a worried voice. 'Watch where you're going, get hold of yourself . . . Woe to him who sows in the flesh, for he will reap corruption, and blessed is he who sows in the spirit, for he will reap eternal life . . .'

Elias shook his head again.

'I don't understand these things. Only priests understand them; besides I'm not in sin, I've hurt no one. Forget about me, Father Porcheddu.'

'You don't understand these things, Elias, but you can imagine the consequences of your sin. Think, think, if this gets out some day. What horror, what tragedy! Think of your mother, think of your father! Think that the sin can't be hidden for long, because where there's smoke there's fire.'

'I'm not in sin,' the other one repeated with obstinate coldness. 'Nothing can happen when there's nothing there.'

Elias was unshakeable. Father Porcheddu left him, desperate to save him; in spite of everything, Elias was deeply moved by this conversation. His was such a horrible happiness, embittered by remorse, by fear, by the horror of sin! Everything that Father Porcheddu said to him he thought over and repeated to himself continually; but he could not or did not try to conquer himself. After the pleasure he would feel all the torment of sorrow, remorse, disgust; but he would return to his sinful happiness in order to escape that pain, that remorse. And in addition, in the saddest moments of his desperation, he began to feel disgust and contempt for Maddalena.

'She is the tempter,' he said to himself after his conversation with Father Porcheddu. 'I am lost because of her. Why did she come? Why did she tempt me? Doesn't that woman think about God, or eternal life?'

Then he regretted that contempt, remembering how much Maddalena loved him and he felt drawn to her by an even deeper tenderness, by a love ever more ardent. Father Porcheddu's words, however, had thrown down good seed; remorse and pain were made more intense in Elias' heart and he began to think again that he must look for peace somewhere other than near Maddalena.

'One day we'll be old,' he once said to her, 'what will we do then? Will God pardon us?'

'Let's not talk about those things!' she said with annoyance. 'Oh, maybe you want to be a priest like you said at the feast of St Francis?'

He started but did not answer, but his disgust and irritation towards Maddalena grew. If she had answered him to the point, showing hope in God's mercy, he would have been moved and would have loved her more. But her mockery and scorn made him hate her for a moment. From that evening they began to have little arguments about one thing or another;

when they were apart Elias was sorry for what he had said, but as soon as he saw Maddalena he began again.

'Listen, Elias,' she finally said to him. 'You are irritated and unfair to me; and after your hot words I often say things I don't mean. We end up not understanding each other any more, while we can't live without each other. It'll be better not to see each other for a while, don't you think? It's much better for us to leave each other for a little . . .'

'No, in fact it's better for us to see each other more often and fight so we'll end up by hating each other and separating forever.'

'Elias!' she said growing pale. 'Why do you talk like that? Why must we hate each other and separate forever?'

'Because we are in mortal sin.'

She became deathly sad.

'And didn't you know it before, Elias Portolu? Now it's too late!'

'Why is it too late?'

'Because I'm the mother of our child . . .'

He also changed colour, and a whirlwind of different feelings overcame him. He covered Maddalena with kisses, talked like a crazy man, asked her pardon, promised her everything she wanted.

They parted, deciding to stay away from each other until the baby was born; and Elias, madly in love, finally felt happier than he had felt for a long time.

VIII

Then it was autumn; the sky became deeper and cooler, the air transparent; huge rains purified the ground and atmosphere. Elias felt he too had plunged into a basin, he seemed even to have become pure again, his thoughts had grown clearer, and for some time his days had been happy.

On these serene days he lay for long hours under a tree looking at the blue sky through the branches, listening to the far away voice of the woods, the bubbling of the stream, the call of birds.

And he continued to think of Maddalena, but differently from the way he had thought of her before; now he loved her chastely, as in the early days, or better, as a husband who thinks of his wife, the mother of his son. And he thought often of this son.

'He'll be a boy,' he said to himself. 'As soon as he grows a little he'll come here with us, with me; I'll

148

always keep him with me. I'll make him love me very much, very much.'

And he felt completely happy; but often a shadow disturbed him: 'And if Pietro wants him with him? He'll think he is his son, he'll take him with him and make him a farmer, he'll love him like a father.'

'No, no!' he then thought. 'I'll tell him: leave me the boy. I'll never get married and I'll leave him everything I have; I'll make him study, I'll make him mine. Pietro will give in and my boy will love me.' Little by little the idea of this boy took hold of him completely; he made extravagant plans and began to think more of him than of Maddalena.

One day Mattia arrived at full speed, bringing to the sheepfold the happy news.

'Papa, brother, Maddalena will have a baby boy; my mother prayed to St Anna, and the child will be a boy.'

He was smiling happily, as though he were the father. Zio Portolu cried a little for joy, and began to praise St Francis, Our Lady of Valverde, Our Lady of Rimedio and who knows how many other saints.

'Ah, the dove! I told him that he couldn't disgrace us by remaining childless. Ah, a little Portolu, the new dove, when will we see him?' he chattered.

'Oh!' Mattia said laughing. 'You'd like him to be born this minute and come to watch the sheep!'

Elias felt his heart pounding, and he was thinking sorrowfully, 'If they only knew!' but deep down he was happy and, strange thing, almost glad for having given this happiness to his family. And like Zio

149

Portolu he couldn't wait until the baby was born.

In the meantime the days went by, the cold, the fog, the snow returned; a very hard winter came, and Elias, who was rather sensitive to the cold, began to feel discomfort at the sheepfold. As he had the year before, he wished for the sweetness of the *focolare* and a comfortable life indoors.

'Oh, what sweetness!' he thought, 'to spend long hours by the fire next to Maddalena!' But now he didn't dream of it as in the year before, with trembling passion. No, he saw her next to a cradle and heard the nostalgic lullaby that reminded him of his infancy. So, without his being able to say why, the rhythm of his heart slowed down day by day. A mysterious force that was no longer remorse or terror, disgust, tiredness or fear was slowly working on him. From afar, on the cold days in the sheepfold, he still yearned to be next to Maddalena, but when he saw her again he no longer felt the terrible happiness of a year before.

He thought: 'Perhaps it's because she is in this condition, but after the baby's born I'll go back to loving her like I did.'

One day, however, Zia Annedda said to Arrita Scada in Elias' presence: 'Elias says he'll never marry; no one wants Mattia because he's simple; so Maddalena will have to give us many children, isn't that right, Arrita Scada? Otherwise who'll be around the *focolare* when we're gone?'

Elias felt an intense disgust, a blow to the heart, thinking about those children who could have been his. Oh, no, one is enough.

'Never, never!' he shouted within himself.

On the first day of Lent he went to Father Porcheddu and confessed. He didn't show the repentance, the sorrow, and the fervour of last year, but he said he had firmly decided not to fall into mortal sin again.

Elias seemed like another person. Father Porcheddu saw clearly that the fire of passion was spent in him, but he looked at him long and thoughtfully and shook his head a few times.

'Now it seems like this to you,' he said, 'but you'll see, if you don't save yourself now you'll be lost again. Take advantage of this moment of grace.'

'What do you mean, Father Porcheddu?'

'Don't you remember what you wanted to do last year? I made the necessary arrangements and it seemed that everything was going to work out all right . . .'

'Ah, I know what you mean,' Elias murmured, lowering his eyes like a boy. 'But now! . . .'

'All right, and now? . . . What does that mean? Haven't you thought about it further?'

'Yes, I've often thought about it; but I think it's too late now, and I'm no longer worthy . . .'

'It's never too late for God's mercy, Elias Portolu. Think it over if you want to save yourself . . .'

Elias, thoughtful, head down, was struck by a memory; he saw himself in the *tanca*, on a grey and silent evening, and saw the stiff figure of Zio Martinu and heard his words again.

'Father Porcheddu,' he said, 'if afterwards, if I

151

became a priest and was still tempted? Wouldn't it be worse?'

'No, Elias Portolu, I know you by now. You'll conquer the temptation, or better, the temptation won't bother you again. Because for you, temptation is that woman, and when she saw you were a priest she would no longer tempt you.'

'Who knows!' said Elias sadly.

'Besides they can send you to a town far away and, if you want, you'll never see her again.'

'Yes, afterwards. But in the meantime!'

'In the meantime? Never fear; you'll go to a seminary and I'll make you study; you'll only be able to go home at certain hours during the day, and if it's what you want, you'll never fall into temptation again. Make your decision, Elias Portolu, don't lose time. Think that we must die, that our life is so short, that we have only one soul and we must save it.' Saying these words Father Porcheddu looked at Elias, almost wanting to frighten him; and in fact he saw him suddenly pale and almost faint; but soon Elias raised his face and his eyes were burning.

'All right then,' he said with deep feeling, 'do what you think best. I trust you, Father Porcheddu. I won't say anything at home until everything is decided.'

'Good, go. I promise you that in eight days everything will be done; in the meantime I advise you to go to church often. Go, my son, and be happy. You'll see that you'll seem to be reborn to another life.'

Elias went away, but couldn't be happy. Ah, no, he

seemed to be dreaming, he no longer felt the childlike, unreasonable joy that he had felt the year before after his confession; quite the opposite, he had become sad, and bitter tears clouded his eyes. Still he was firm in his decision, but he was sad just because of that decision. Now it was no longer a dream, it was reality; and in the first moment of his resolution, he was unable to separate himself from the past without feeling his heart break. It was goodbye to everything that made up his life; it was his life itself that was going away, with its habits, joys, sorrows, passions, errors and pleasures.

For several days he lived with the bitterness of this farewell; sadness gripped him particularly in the *tanca* until he felt cold and indifferent to everything that was not part of his farewell to things and to the places where he had loved and suffered so much.

'I'll never see this again, I'll never do that again,' he thought, and a knot tightened in his throat. But his decision was firm, and the more time passed the more he grew accustomed to the idea of leaving everything and beginning a new life. Little by little, after he had secretly said farewell to every little thing, to every tree and rock, to the animals and men, his mind became clearer and he began to envisage the future.

Returning to town he went to church and stayed many hours there, attending the religious services with intense devotion. The sound of the organ, the solemn lamentation of the liturgical songs, the priest's vestments all enchanted him, and thinking that one day he too would sing those prayers that gave him such sweet torment and that he would wear those holy vestments, he forgot the past and felt happy. But when he re-entered the house he was once more troubled, especially in Maddalena's presence.

'What will she say when she finds out?' he kept thinking. It seemed he no longer loved her, especially now that she had become nearly shapeless, her face yellow and swollen; but he felt bound to her by an indissoluble knot that he was afraid to break.

'What will she think? What will she say? Will she despair? Ah, maybe it will hurt her; it'll probably be better to wait.' And he kept thinking, tenderly, of the child that was to come, but for his part he was glad of the decision; his new state would not keep him from loving the child. In fact now more than ever he could take the child with him, bring him up, make him a respectable man and provide a future for him.

But one day he spoke to Father Porcheddu and he shook his head: 'Don't even think of it,' he said, 'because you do yourself no good by thinking about it. In the first place, the child is still in the Lord's mind. But even when it's born and growing up you must stay away, because it would always be a dangerous bond between you and *her*. A priest must not have children or wife or family; he must not think of the riches of earthly things; he is the bride of the church and his children are poverty, duty, good work. Think it over, Elias Portolu; if you still feel attached to the things of the world, don't take the step you feel you should: you must think only about the salvation of your soul and nothing else.'

154

'You want to make me a saint,' Elias said smiling, but deep down he felt that Father Porcheddu was right and it saddened him to have to say farewell to his dream of being a father. But not even this deterred him from the decision he had made.

The eight days passed; Father Porcheddu's papers were favourably received; the monsignor bishop was very interested in this young shepherd with the wish to dedicate himself to God, and he would admit him immediately to the seminary at half cost. Following the advice of Father Porcheddu, Elias wrote a thank-you letter to the bishop that made the monsignor even more enthusiastic.

'The monsignor wants to meet you, Elias Portolu; now you just have to tell your family.'

'Ah!' said Elias with a sigh. 'I'm afraid . . .'

'Afraid of what?'

'That it will hurt that woman. If we could just wait!'

Father Porcheddu shook his head.

'You want to wait? You are still attached to the things of this world? Ah, ah, I don't like this!'

'All right then,' Elias said firmly, 'I want to show you that I'm not attached to anything. I'll tell them the news at home this very day.'

'Is your father in town?'

'Yes.'

'And your brother Pietro?'

'He is too.'

'Good. After dinner tell those in the house; I'll come and we'll all discuss it.'

'I don't know how to thank you!' exclaimed Elias with gratitude. 'Only God can repay you.'

'Good, good; we'll speak to God about it another time; now go in peace.'

Elias went away, but couldn't go home until dinner time; his heart felt heavy, his throat tight. Ah, the reality of his dream was coming closer, it already surrounded him, crushed him, tore him violently from the world, from his youth, from pleasure, from his family, from the life he had lived up to this time. And it gave him enormous sorrow; but not even for a minute did it occur to him to turn back.

He went home and ate dinner, distracted, with his eyes always on the door; and he jumped every time he heard the noise of footsteps in the lane. Maddalena was watching him and couldn't keep from asking what was wrong and whom he was expecting.

'Someone,' he answered. 'As a matter of fact, I beg you all to stay here, since this person wants to talk with you.'

'Even with me?' Maddalena asked. 'Who is it? Who is it?'

'With everyone. You'll see who it is.'

They bombarded him with questions, but he made no reply and went out into the courtyard. Maddalena was gripped by an uneasiness she didn't try to hide even from Pietro, and she also began to look at the door and listen when anyone came along the lane.

'Who could this person be?' she said every once in a while as though to herself. For some time she had been well aware of the change in Elias, and the fear that he might be in love with another woman and was thinking of getting married made her suffer with jealousy.

'He wants to get married,' she was thinking that day, 'and the person he is expecting must be the go-between who is coming to ask our permission to let him ask her for Elias. Ah, must this day come? And so soon! Can't he even wait for his child? God, my God, help me, give me strength, you who are merciful. Don't make me die, don't punish me before my time.'

Deep suffering marked her pale face and eyelids, those wide eyelids lowered in resigned sorrow became violet.

When Elias re-entered with Father Porcheddu and looked at her he grew afraid; he too became pale and felt a deathly cold in his veins.

But Father Porcheddu was singing softly to himself, looking around, greeting everyone with jokes and clumsy bows. He wanted to stay in the kitchen even though Zia Annedda kindly pressed them to go up to Maddalena's room.

'Well then, how is it going, Zio Portolu?'

'On two legs like a chicken, Father Porcheddu!'

'And your sons, are your sons good boys? Still doves?'

'Ah, yes,' exclaimed Zio Portolu, widening his little red eyes. 'Like my sons, there are a few of them, thanks to St Francis.'

Elias forced himself to smile, but Father Porcheddu saw distress in his face, and after a little chatter he looked at Maddalena, winked, and said: 'And soon we will have another dove, won't we? Ha, ha, St Francis loves you well, Zio Portolu: all God's grace is with you. And now listen to me: what would you say if your son Elias became a priest?'

Everyone was stunned, because if Father Porcheddu talked like that the thing was already decided. Who would have expected it? Maddalena raised her eyes and a fleeting blush brightened her face. After what she had feared, Father Porcheddu's words seemed glad news to her. Elias was lost to her, but she could still resign herself to it since he wouldn't have another woman.

Elias noticed her joy. Then he calmed down and observed the impression that the priest's question had made on his family. It was as though someone had told a joke. Pietro was smiling. Zia Annedda, sitting near Father Porcheddu with her intent face and straining ears, was smiling; Zio Portolu's wild face was smiling.

Elias realized that what Father Porcheddu had said made his family so happy they thought they were dreaming; and suddenly even he felt such a rush of joy that he began to laugh like a child.

IX

Two years went by. People stopped murmuring, laughing, wondering at seeing Elias Portolu, the ex-shepherd, dressed like a seminarist. Anyway he didn't seem at all like a young man of twenty-six, much less an ex-shepherd; seclusion had made his hands and face white again; his pearly-pale, shaven face was like an adolescent's.

In the big religious services, when he wore the lace tunic tied with a large blue ribbon, he seemed a melancholy angel with a crease of great, but sweet, sadness alongside his pale rose mouth; many of the young girls of the town, and even some young women, looked at him a little too long with great interest. But he did not notice; his greenish eyes were lost in distant visions. What did he see then when the organ groaned and the liturgical chants rose with a nostalgic lamentation for lost good and with the invocation grieving for unknown good? He saw the past, the *tanca*, the solitude; did he remember his passion? Yes, he saw and remembered everything, and he grieved at being powerless to detach himself from the past as he had hoped and believed, and what attached him still to the sorrow and joy of human passions was the continual vision of that young woman kneeling at the back of the church, among the spreading purple of the crowd of townspeople. It was Maddalena, beautiful and resplendent in her bride's costume; in her arms she held the baby covered by a scarlet *mantiglia* edged with blue silk; and when his mother dangled before his little face the amulets of silver and coral that hung from his little neck, the baby lifted his rosy little hands and smiled, half opening his bright green eyes.

Elias saw this smiling creature continually before him, and loved him with a sad tenderness, and loving the baby loved the mother, and often suffered in the vain struggle against his worldly loves.

His natural intelligence, in the meanwhile, was being developed. Two years of tireless study, of continual reading, of goodwill, had put him on the level of the seminarists who had been studying many years before he began. Gradually he had become accustomed to the confined life, to blind obedience, to discipline: things that at first had nearly suffocated him. The past seemed like a dream to him, but a dream to which he had clung tenaciously.

He felt sad, especially on the days when he went home, where Zia Annedda greeted him with tender awe; he carefully avoided Maddalena's eyes and was

160

afraid to touch the baby. Or if they made him caress him he did it timidly; but he started at the sight of him, and the desire to take him in his arms and kiss him, make him smile, to look at his first teeth, to grasp both his hands, both his little feet in one of his hands, wrung his heart.

'No, no,' he repeated to himself, 'you have to overcome.'

Maddalena's presence also, never reproaching him but often looking at him in sorrowful tenderness, often stirred his blood. She was more attractive than ever, entirely taken up with her little son for whose life she seemed solely to live. And Elias was unable to separate her from the boy.

He felt that if he had remained free – since he already felt tied to God, although he had not yet received the first orders – he would have undoubtedly fallen again. As it stood he was able to overcome even his thoughts, but the struggle was often agonizing and left him half dead with anguish. And so these days he felt very sad, and despaired of life and of himself; however, he never had a moment of rebellion or regret for the decision he had made.

At times his strength failed; tormenting dreams, asleep and awake, attacked him worse than any temptation. Almost every night he dreamed of the past, the *tanca*, the sheepfold, the little house, Maddalena, and often the child also. He always seemed still to be a shepherd and free; however, a grey oppression and a painful memory he could never quite manage to grasp made these dreams nightmares. And

161

yet it was not these dreams that caused him such anxiety, but the wide-awake dreams, sweet and ruinous dreams that locked him in insidious circles. 'No! No! No!' he kept repeating, chasing away the vain desires and fatal images, and he would begin to pray and study; but almost always, even though chased away a hundred times, a hundred times the sad dreams returned.

One night he was studying the Epistle of St Paul to the Romans; it was a clear, moonlit night in April. Through the open window wafted a breeze suffused with sweetness, and a very bright star could be seen blinking in the crystalline sky. Elias felt sadder than usual; life tempted and spoke to him and assailed him with the pure breath of that April night; inexpressible memories returned to mind, and with the rebirth of spring, something new and disquieting seemed to be germinating in his blood.

'No, no, no . . .' he repeated to himself, shaking his head as though to chase the troublesome thoughts away. 'I have to forget everything; study, go on, Elias Portolu.' He held his head in his hands and immersed himself in his reading. All around was a profound silence, and in the distance, very far off, almost out of the deep countryside, wavered a melancholy song. Elias read, re-read, meditated, memorized the verses.

. . . Let love be without hypocrisy. Abhor that which is evil; cleave to that which is good.

. . . diligent not slothful; fervent in spirit; serving the Lord;

... rejoicing in hope; patient in tribulation, continuing
steadfastly in prayer;
   ... Bless them which persecute you: bless and curse not.
   ... Render to no man evil for evil. Take thought for
things honourable in the sight of all men.
   ... Vengeance belongeth to me; I will recompense, saith
the Lord.
   ... Be not overcome by evil, but overcome evil with good.'

How proud and sweet was the Apostle's voice! It
was like rumbling thunder and like the pure voice of a
bubbling fountain in the quiet evening; but it came
from too far off, from too high, like the rumble of
thunder, like the murmuring fountain heard in a
dream. Elias listened to it; and he felt all enveloped
and refreshed as from a fragrant sudarium; but,
unfortunately, it was a flimsy sudarium that the
breath of that soft April night was enough to tear.

The far-off Sardinian song[13] was a little less distant;
from the melancholy choir a harmonious tenor voice
rose. All the voluptuousness and sweetness of that
moonlit night trembled in it. Elias raised his head,
struck by a sudden enchantment. Where had he heard
that voice? An almost physical memory made him
start. He remembered having lived another night like
that, of having heard that song, of having been sad as
he was now. Where? When? How? He got up, leaned
against the window under the pure ray of the moon at
its zenith. The breeze carried distant fragrances; he
shuddered and remembered the night he cried
passionately at the feet of St Francis.

163

The Apostle's voice spoke no more; the veil had fallen: what was eternity, death, vanity of every human passion, good, evil, perfection, eternal life before the fleeting joy of that love song? Elias was conquered; life grasped him again. He fell on his knees before the window, under the moon, and cried like a child caught up in the greatest delirium of desperation.

An incoherent prayer rose from his weeping.

'Lord, you see how weak and vile I am; have pity on me, my God, pardon me, give me peace, tear my heart from my breast. I am a man, I can't conquer myself; why did you make me so weak, oh Lord? I have always suffered in my life, and when I was overcome by my weak nature looking for happiness, I sinned, I trampled on your precepts. I have been more pagan and wicked than the Gentiles; but I have suffered so much, my God; and I am still suffering so much I can't take any more. My God, my God, my God!' he continued, sobbing, with his contorted face bathed in salty tears, 'have mercy on me, pardon me, help me, give my heart peace . . . give me a little good . . . a little sweetness: don't I have a right to it, my God? Aren't I a human creature? If I have sinned, pardon me, if you are merciful, if you are great, Lord, pardon me and give me a little good, a little joy . . .'

Gradually his tears were exhausted, and the outburst made him feel better, calmer. Once the excess of desperation passed, he was ashamed to have cried, but he thought: 'My father says that cowards cry; and that a Sardinian, a Nuorese, must not cry; but it does much good! Otherwise sometimes a person would break!'

He was also afraid and ashamed of his prayer that was almost a challenge to God; and he asked pardon and resigned himself; but the next morning he had a very strong reaction of fear, surprise, pain and also joy, when they came to tell him that his brother Pietro had returned from the country with a bad kidney inflammation, and that his condition was very serious.

'If he dies I'll be able to marry Maddalena!' he thought at once.

Had God granted his prayer? Oh, no! He drew back frightened by his blasphemy before such a monstrous image of a God that he had created in his fantasy at that moment. It wasn't possible.

'How vile I am!' he thought, going quickly to his house. 'No, I'll never save myself. I am evil.'

He anguished more over his evil thoughts than over Pietro's illness; and he was repentant and berated himself. And yet when he arrived at his home and learned how his brother had come home ill the day before, he felt sorry, as much as he was tempted by the strange idea that God had heard his prayer.

Pietro's condition was truly serious; he moaned continually, his ashen face contorted by intense suffering. Three days before he had had to run a great distance to reach one of his lost oxen; anxiety, fatigue, heat, a predisposition to this weakness, had brought him down. His feet were swollen and bloody, his hands scratched by brambles and stones.

A heavy anxiety ruled over the Portolus' house; Maddalena cried sincerely; Zia Annedda had lit two lamps and said the *parole verdi*; and the green words

165

had replied that Pietro must die.

Terrible days followed for Elias. He would go to his brother, look at him, circle the room silently wringing his hands, dismayed by not being able to do anything to save him; he never turned to look at Maddalena or the boy, and he went away in despair. He prayed fervently for hours for the sick man to get well. But often, even in the fervour of his prayers, he would start and his blood would freeze: oh, what monster attacked him? Why, as soon as he forgot for one instant, did that monster whisper words of joy to him, give him guilty desires, continually show him the image of his dead, buried brother?

'It's the demon,' he thought one evening, 'but he will not win, no, he'll never win again! All right, let Pietro die, if he must; yes, as horrible as that would be, Satan, I now want my brother to die to show you that you'll never conquer me. Never again! Never again! I'm stronger than you, Satan; my body is weak and you can break it, but you'll never win over my soul ever again.'

That evening Pietro died. Elias closed his eyes, made the sign of the cross over his face, helped Zia Annedda wash and dress the body.

Then he stayed up all night with his dead brother. Every once in a while he got up, bent over his face, and looked at him for a long time, with the foolish hope that he was not dead, that he would move and rise up from one moment to another.

But the bearded, grey face with closed eyes remained as still as a fearful bronze mask. Elias felt, perhaps for

166

the first time in his life – since he had never seen a cadaver so close and for such a long time – all the inescapable grandeur of death. He remembered Pietro alive, smiling; oh, the slightest thing was enough to throw him down there, unmoving, mute forever! Forever! 'Tomorrow at this time even these remains will disappear from the world!' he was thinking; and he couldn't convince himself that everything ended like this, that even he, his parents, his brother, Maddalena and their child would be gone one day. Then he fell on his knees at the foot of the bed, and his sorrow was changed into comfort.

'Yes, everything ends,' he thought. 'And we'll never suffer again. Why get so upset? Everything ends: only the soul remains. We must save it.'

And more than ever he felt strong against temptation and evil; then he turned to memories of his brother alive; to their childhood and youth, to the mortal offence he had done him, and he was grief-stricken and sobs closed his throat.

'Now that he is dead,' he asked himself, 'will he know how I offended him? And will he forgive me?'

But this question led to other memories; he saw Maddalena again in that same room where the dead man now lay, and a sudden sweetness of thought insidiously overcame him that now he could love her without sin; but he immediately rejected this temptation, and bending over the face of the corpse again he immersed himself in the vision of death. In this way the night passed.

At dawn he slept a little; and he dreamed of Pietro

167

alive, coming to the *tanca* (as he was always doing when Elias was still a shepherd). Pietro came on horseback, and his face was grey and his eyes were closed just like the cadaver's.

'What's wrong?' Elias asked, terrified.

'The boy is dead; I came to tell you,' Pietro answered. 'Go into town, because you have to bury him.'

Elias felt so much fear and anguish that he made an effort to wake himself up, but upon awakening he still felt as distressed as in the dream. It was day. He heard the child cry, and thought sorrowfully: 'Must he also die? Is the dream a warning? Misfortunes never come alone; and I believe in dreams.'

By now it seemed that all misfortunes were possible, near, inevitable; and overcome by a great sadness, he went to see little Berte.

The boy was crying. Maddalena, already in widow's clothes (and the black dress made her even lovelier, young and fresh as she was), tried to calm him, talking to him in a quiet voice. Many relatives had already arrived; the house was plunged entirely in darkness.

Elias advanced silently, almost furtively, into the faint light of the room.

'What's the matter?' he asked, bending over the child. 'Why is he crying?' he asked Maddalena.

Berte looked at him with big tearful eyes, and quietened down, with his little mouth open and quivering. Then he began to cry again; Maddalena also raised her eyes to Elias and her mouth was also quivering.

'Quiet, quiet, sweet child,' he said in a trembling voice, rocking the child in his arms. 'Be good, here's Zio Elias who doesn't want you to cry . . .' But suddenly she bent her face over the child's shoulders and began to cry disconsolately.

'All right, Maddalena, what is this?' Elias asked, beside himself

Then he moved away as though pushed by an invisible hand. That scene entered his blood; he felt that Maddalena's tears were not only for the death of her husband, and her look, always tender and ardent, penetrated his heart.

'Oh,' he thought, 'if the temptation is so strong while my brother's body is still here, practically still warm, what will it be afterwards? No, no, no!' he resolved angrily. 'I will overcome. I must overcome and I will overcome.'

But the terrible struggle had begun. The first, the second, the third day of the funeral, the condolences, the Sardinian mourning ceremonies,[14] went by like a bad dream.

At last Elias was alone in his cell, on his little bed, tired, worn out. Always on his mind was the night he read the Epistle of St Paul, and the memory of his desperate prayer returned like a regret.

'I've been harshly punished for it!' he thought. 'And yet, who knows the ways of the Lord? If He had wanted to grant my wish? If that were my way? Why don't I have the right to worldly happiness? Am I not a man like the others?'

And the insidious dream overcame him. The pure and fragrant spring air filled his cell, and from the window a sky appeared in the background so deep, so blue! Wasn't he a man like the others? He had sinned! All right, and what man does not sin? And who is condemned to eternal punishment for it?

'That's it, that's it; I'll leave the seminary with the excuse that my brother is dead and they need me at home now. People will talk a little, but what don't they talk about? In a year no one will say anything, and then! . . .' Oh, what sweetness! Was ever such sweetness possible? Yes, it was finally possible!

'Why am I so stupid as to hesitate an instant?' he asked, marvelling at himself and at the vain torments he gave himself. He felt his heart full of joy; but suddenly his heart emptied, and he plunged again into deep despair.

'No! No! No! Why am I raving like this? Is this the way to overcome temptation, Elias Portolu? Are these your vows? No, no, no; I will overcome; get back, Satan, I will conquer you, I will conquer you!'

He squeezed his fists as for a real fight. And so passed the hours, days, nights, and months.

One day they told him that he would soon take the first holy orders. He was not gladdened, nor was he saddened. By now he seemed to have acquired experience and could no longer delude himself. He remembered the early days of his love, when he had hoped that the marriage of Pietro and Maddalena

170

would be enough to heal his passion. Instead! . . .

'No, I don't want to delude myself,' he thought. 'I'll always be a man subject to passions. No, salvation is not in the barriers between us and sin, but in our strength and in our will.'

When he went home to share his news, fortunately he found all his family together; even Mattia was there (the Portolus had a servant now that Zio Berte and his son were unable to do all the work in the sheepfold and fields) and the relative Jacu Farre, who came often to the house after Pietro's death.

Jacu Farre was a *principale* owning herds, land, horses and beehives, and he was a bachelor; he had taken a great interest in Pietro's orphan, and the Portolus treated him with kid gloves, in the hope that he might leave his earthly goods to the child. Therefore, Elias found him with his family; he held Berte on his knee and said to him: 'Let's ride a horse; let's go to the festival, eh, Berteddu?'

The boy laughed. Elias was put out; he looked at Farre, who in spite of his plumpness was a handsome man. He looked at Berte, at Maddalena, and felt a surge of jealousy, but he soon controlled himself and told his news. For the Portolus, and especially for Zia Annedda, whose grief over Pietro's death had aged her ten years, making her completely deaf, Elias' good news was like a ray of sunshine.

'St Francis be praised!' said Zio Portolu. 'I've been waiting for this day; if I hadn't had this hope I'd have killed myself. Oh, all of you can smile! You can smile, Jacu Farre! Oh, you don't know what Zio Portolu's heart is made of !' And he sighed many times.

Elias became gloomy; he thought: 'My father means it; if I left the seminary he couldn't bear the pain.'

Only Maddalena didn't seem gladdened by the news. Her wide eyelids lowered with a greater expression of resigned sorrow, she did not look once at Elias, but he was not deceived a moment about her feelings.

'She still loves me,' he thought as he went away. 'Jacu Farre is courting her in vain. She is mine, mine alone. She wants to see me, she'll do anything to talk to me, to get me alone, I'm sure of that. What shall I do?'

He didn't know, just as he didn't know when and how Maddalena would be able to talk to him; but meanwhile he was waiting, and this waiting prepared him for the struggle, or at least it fortified him against his weakness if he was taken unawares. If they told him that someone was looking for him, he would feel his heart pounding, and think: 'It's her!' and then, seeing that it was not her, he would breathe freely and become sad at the same time. If he went home, he would be afraid of meeting Maddalena alone. He would enter cautiously, and then feel irritated when he saw she was not alone.

'Because it has to end!' he said to himself as an excuse. 'We must talk and put an end to it once and for all.'

But much time went by and Maddalena did not bother him.

'She is resigned. So much the better! Who knows? Maybe I'm deceiving myself, maybe she thinks more of Jacu Farre than of me!' he told himself; and he seemed to be happy about it, but deep down felt a strange and groundless sorrow.

One October afternoon, however, two or three days before the planned ceremony of the orders, while he was studying in his cell, they came to say he had a visitor.

'It's her!' he thought, disturbed.

It wasn't her, but a neighbour's young boy, sent by her.

'Tell Father Elias' – that's what they called him – 'to go home immediately, because he's needed there.'

'Is it mamma?' Elias asked.

'I don't know.'

'Is the boy ill?'

'I don't know.'

'All right; I'll come right away.'

And he went with his heart gripped by foreboding. Maddalena was, in fact, alone in the house. Zia Annedda had gone to the country, little Berte was sleeping. The lane was deserted and all around the house was the sweetness, the infinite peace of the hazy autumn afternoon.

As soon as Maddalena saw Elias she became very agitated and felt that she had prepared a long discourse full of persuasive logic in vain. The time when she had gone to the *tanca* and had won Elias with a kiss was now far away. Now she was afraid, and perhaps now calculation spoke more strongly than passion. In any case, she was agitated and confused. She had Elias sit down, she served the coffee, ready

173

for him as always, then without looking at him she asked:

'So the ceremony is on Sunday?'

'You didn't know that?'

'Yes, I knew it.'

Silence.

'Why did you get me to come here?' he asked finally.

'Why?' she said, as though questioning herself. 'Oh, wait, the boy's waking up. Ah, my Berteddu, be quiet. I'm coming, I'm coming. Here's Zio Elias.' She got up, and went to the child and brought him in with her. Elias was afraid.

'Elias,' she began, 'perhaps you can imagine what I want to tell you.' He shook his head. 'Doesn't this innocent creature tell you anything? Doesn't your conscience tell you anything? Examine it; you still have time. Won't God, who sees everything, be happier if you become the father of this innocent child, instead of doing what you are about to do?'

She stopped speaking, looking at him, and waiting for his reply. Elias put his trembling hand on the boy's little head, unconsciously caressing him.

'What do you want me to say? It's too late now, Maddalena,' he murmured.

'No, it's not too late, it's not too late.'

'It's too late, I tell you. The scandal would be terrible; they would say I was crazy.'

'Ah,' she said bitterly, 'the evil tongues in the world keep you from listening to your conscience?'

'But my conscience tells me to follow the way that

174

I'm about to follow, Maddalena!' he said, serious, never raising his eyes, continually caressing little Berte. 'Anyway, tell me, if I took off this habit and married you, could we ever say that this child is my son?'

'Before the world, Elias! Before the world he'll never be your son, but you could treat him like your son all the same!'

'I'll love him just the same, and take care of him the same. No one, in my new state, will stop me from doing my duty by him.'

'No, no,' she said, beginning to give herself up to despair, bowing and shaking her head, 'no, no, it's not the same, it's not the same thing!'

'It is the same thing, I tell you, Maddalena . . .'

'That's what you say, but it's not the same thing. And then!' she burst out, raising her head boldly. 'Me, Elias! Me! You don't think of me?'

'I can't,' he murmured.

'You can't? And why not, Elias? You still have time! Is it possible you don't remember anything?'

'I can't remember. And anyway, I'll say it again, it's too late.'

'It's not too late, it's not too late . . .' she repeated, twisting her hands, made desperate by not knowing how to say the words she had prepared.

She was shrewd enough to realize that Elias was perturbed, that he had paled, that his hand shook on Berte's head, that it would only take a little daring to win him over. She had the desire to stand up, put her arms around his neck and talk to him as she had talked to him in the *tanca*. But a greater power held her back and almost kept her from looking at him. She felt as shy and uneasy as a girl in conversation with her first boyfriend. And the conversation proceeded miserably and ended miserably.

Maddalena repeated in a hundred different ways things already said; she reminded Elias of the past, she told him she would always love him, that she would live and die thinking of him; but by now she no longer had a touching passionate tone, and all her words and her reasons were not equal to the look that had conquered Elias in the *tanca*. He heard all this and was able to control himself.

They separated without even touching hands; but when Elias was alone he felt that his had been too easy and poor a victory.

'If she had tempted me perhaps I would have fallen again,' he thought. 'But because she remained cold, I did too. Perhaps, now that she has begun, she will return again to the assault, because she loves me. It's not just to give Berte a father, but to have my love again that she tempts me.'

He felt sad, troubled, weak; and yet he did not give up hoping in God's grace. With the pleasure with which a fanatic whips his body, he wanted Maddalena to come after him and tempt him again, strongly, in order to suffer and try his strength of resistance.

X

Maddalena did not try to tempt him again. He received the first orders, continued studying and was soon consecrated a priest and could say mass. His family celebrated this occasion like a wedding. Relatives and friends brought presents as though to a bridegroom; sheep and lambs were slaughtered, a banquet was prepared, songs improvised for the young priest were sung. Zio Portolu wore everything new, oiled his hair, refashioned his braids; he was now listening to the extemporaneous poets' competition, holding on his knee little Berte, who rested his melancholy little head on his grandfather's chest.

'What's wrong, my little lamb?' Zia Annedda asked, bending over the little one. 'Are you sleepy?'

The child shook his head; his big green eyes were sad. Zia Annedda went to get a little bird-shaped biscuit made of flour and honey, and bending over her grandson once more she gave it to him.

'Take it; here's a little bird; don't get sleepy.'

The boy took it listlessly, without raising his head from his grandfather's chest, and drew the bird's beak to his mouth, but didn't eat it.

'Are you sleepy?' asked Zio Portolu, looking at him. 'Didn't you sleep last night, my little bird? Come on, listen to the nice songs! When you grow up you'll sing like that. I'll take you to the *tanca* on a horse and we'll sing together.'

But the little boy, who was always excited by the idea of going to the *tanca*, didn't react. At dinner he didn't want to eat, and he clung to his grandfather, continuing to rest his head on his chest.

'I think your son is sick,' Farre yelled to Maddalena.

Father Elias started, looked at the child and immediately remembered the dream he had had the night he sat up with Pietro's body. Maddalena caressed Berte, questioned him, took him in her arms and carried him to his little bed where Elias once slept.

'He was sleepy and now he's asleep,' she said when she came back. But Father Elias did not relax. He would have liked to go and check on the boy, but instead he couldn't move and had to hide his anxiety.

He listened to the singers, smiled slightly when certain verses were well done, but did not speak, did not laugh. He saw Farre, that fat rich relative who panted when he talked, going and coming through the house, giving orders, taking a hand in everything as though he were in charge, often speaking to Maddalena; and he felt jealous, and noticing this

178

jealousy made him annoyed with himself, but he kept silent.

After dinner he went to his son almost furtively. He bent over him and watched for a long time, and seeing him sleeping sweetly, with his little mouth half open, with the bird biscuit in his little hands, he felt a rush of tenderness and kissed him devoutly. As he stood up he remembered the day and night of Maddalena's marriage, and the sickness and pain that he had suffered on that bed.

'Things of the world!' he thought. 'Who would ever have believed that these things would happen?'

As he went into the kitchen he heard Farre talking about the boy with Maddalena who was busy preparing the coffee.

'You aren't taking care of him,' he was saying to her. 'Can't you see how ill he is? Is that the face of a well child? No. I'll get the doctor to come and you'll see I'm right.'

'What does it matter to him?' Elias said to himself, with bitterness and jealousy. 'It's up to me to take care of him and not Farre.'

He went out into the courtyard where the poets were starting up their singing again, and sat down next to his father. He appeared to be listening to the extemporaneous competition,[15] but he kept thinking about Farre, Maddalena and the boy. Growing sad and irritable, he became aware of a new desire of his: that Maddalena remain a widow. He had never before realized that he would no longer have any authority over the boy if she should remarry.

179

'She will marry Farre,' he was thinking, 'and I won't be able to show love for my son any longer. I won't be able to kiss and hold him as much as I would like.' And his thoughts wandered into the future, to things far removed from the ministry he had entered into that day.

The celebration over, back again in the seminary, Elias was aware of all his vain thoughts, jealousies, sadnesses felt throughout the day, and a strong self-dislike overtook him.

'It's useless, it's useless,' he thought, tossing and turning on his bed. 'Flesh is attached to bone, and I'll never detach myself from the things of this world. I'll always be a bad priest, just as I was a bad layman, because I'm not a good man. That's all there is to it.'

In the meanwhile, what he predicted came to pass. Farre asked for the hand of Maddalena, and immediately began to concern himself with the child as his own. He got the doctor to come, and after the doctor declared that the boy was anaemic, the big man bought the medicine and whatever was necessary for little Berte's health. Father Elias watched and kept quiet, but jealousy was gnawing at him inside. Many times when he was alone, and even in church, he surprised himself by thinking of that large figure of a ruddy, healthy man, slow talking, panting as he talked, and he hated him.

One day Farre invited him to his sheepfold.

'Zio Portolu will come, too,' he said, 'and we'll bring the boy. It'll do him good and we'll enjoy ourselves.'

180

At first Elias was impetuously going to refuse, then he controlled himself and accepted.

But he suffered much during that trip. Farre took the boy with him on his horse, in front on the saddle, and Berteddu leaned his little head on his chest and asked him a hundred questions when he saw a cawing crow in flight, a sparrow rise out of the scrub, a bush full of scarlet berries, an oak green with acorns. Farre explained everything patiently, and every once in a while gave him a kiss.

'See, that is a wild pear; look, look it has more fruit than leaves; well then, do you like wild pears, little one, eh, eh? And those long grey things that seem like candelabra? Do you know what they are? They're stalks of fox cane, good for making pipe stems. The shepherds make pipes with it. Oh, shepherds aren't like gentlemen, you know, who go to market and buy nice ready-made things. The shepherds make do. And you want to be a shepherd, eh?'

'Yes, I'll be a shepherd,' the boy said lazily, 'and I'll make a pipe with that cane over there.'

'Oh, no, oh, no! Did you hear him, Portolu, the boy wants to be a shepherd! Don't we want him to be a doctor instead?'

It was just talk; yet Elias, riding next to Farre, was childishly bothered by it. What did that outsider have to do with his child's future? No, no, he would never permit him to interfere in the life and destiny of his son.

But this, too, was a dream; reality was already dawning on him with Zio Portolu's words to little

Berte: 'Ah, you want to be a shepherd, little one? And why do you want to be a shepherd? Don't you know that shepherds often sleep out in the open and suffer from the cold? See Zio Elias? He's become a priest; because if he'd stayed a shepherd he'd be dead from the cold. No, you'll be a doctor, not a shepherd. Eh, you won't be the one to decide! There's Zio Farre to keep you on the straight path, and if you do something wrong, Zio Farre won't stand by.'

'What's that?' asked Berteddu, pointing to a tree, without listening to his grandfather.

But Elias had heard them, those powerful words, and he felt struck to his innermost being.

From that day his jealousy grew like a disease. In vain he tried to control it, in vain he thought: 'Jacu Farre will have children, and then he will forget and perhaps stop loving mine. Then Berte will be all mine. I'll take him into my house, I'll keep him on a straight path, I'll make him happy.'

No, no. They were all dreams. The present was pressing on, reality was difficult. Elias suffered; and it was a pain altogether different from the others felt up to that time, but no less profound. He despaired again and repeated the same lamentation: 'I'll never find peace; I'm damned. Whatever I do is wrong. Perhaps I was wrong not to listen to Maddalena; perhaps God wanted me to find a haven from sin instead of devoting myself to Him unworthily. Ah, Father Porcheddu, you were right. Sin is a rock we can never lift off our backs; and I'm damned to the weight of eternal pain because I sinned gravely.'

182

So his days continued to go by in melancholy and torment. Oh, this was not the quiet and holy life that he had dreamed about! In the meantime, from one day to the next, he expected to be sent to some vacated parish in one of the nearby villages. He knew it, and was already suffering just thinking of the distance. With him far away, Farre would marry Maddalena and be in complete possession of the child. It was all over, all finished! But no, no, it wasn't all over. No, he knew that from afar he would continually be thinking of his son, torturing himself with tenderness, desire, jealously, and perhaps he would leave to begin a new life of passions and pain, much different from the life it was his duty to lead.

Every day he went to his home, and tried to befriend the boy more than usual, bringing him sweets, playing with him, spoiling him. He realized that this was a weakness, even a pettiness, since he was compelled to do it not by his paternal love, but by his need to keep Berte from becoming attached to Farre; yet he was unable to do otherwise.

However, he saw with sorrow that Berte remained more or less indifferent, indolent, and silent; he almost never ate the sweets, quickly tired of the toys and play, and became annoyed at the slightest thing. Anyway, he was the same with everyone; and Elias realized that the little one was ill, and it hurt him to see him like this and not be able to make him well.

He got the doctor to come – not the one Farre consulted – and felt a sad satisfaction when the new doctor declared the boy to be affected by a latent illness that was not anaemia, and ordered different medication.

'You see?' Elias said to Maddalena with evil triumph showing in his eyes.

'I see!' she replied sadly, preoccupied only with the boy's condition.

The new doctor and the new medicine, however, did not stop the latent inflammation in the delicate tissues from eventually erupting. One day Father Elias found Berte lying in his little bed in the downstairs bedroom; the boy had a high fever and was delirious, with big wandering eyes and burning face. Maddalena was watching over him, distressed and desperate, and Zia Annedda had resorted to her brand of medicine, invoking as many saints as you could wish for, but all perfectly useless.

Zia Annedda had a special relic for curing fever. She passed it over the child's burning body and fervently recited different prayers to God, to the Holy Spirit, to Our Lady of Pity, to Our Lady of Remedy, to Mary of Valverde, to Mary of the Mountain, to Mary of Miracles, to the Holy Saints, to St Basil, to St Lucia, to the Holy Blood, to the Holy Innocents; but the fever only rose higher.

The first doctor was called back; he said that the child's condition was very serious but not desperate if typhus did not develop. A very pale Elias stood by the little window listening. At that point he saw Farre coming down the lane and instinctively he clenched his fists.

'He is coming, here he is!' he thought. 'He is

184

coming just to make me unhappy! Maybe the boy will die, and I won't be able to come to his little bed, I won't be able to give him his final caresses, his final care, while he'll be allowed to do everything. Here he comes! Oh, well, I'll go away; otherwise, if he comes in here and goes to my dying boy, I won't be responsible for my actions.'

He went away, in fact, with the doctor; in the courtyard he met a sad looking Farre who asked about the boy's condition.

'He's not well; leave him in peace with his mother!' Elias said roughly.

Farre looked at him a little surprised, but said nothing.

The doctor invited Elias to take a walk down the road; the young priest went along gladly; but while the other talked, Elias was looking far off towards the end of the valley, lost in a sorrowful dream. He saw Farre sitting by the little boy's bed, and Maddalena sad and pale bent over the sick child, watching his growing suffering. The plump fiancé was comforting her, then he reached out and caressed the little one and spoke lovingly to him.

Meanwhile the doctor was talking about a fat, rosy girl he had encountered at the fountain.

'They say that girl's Farre's lover. What hips! But not such a good figure, really. But is it true she's his lover? Have you heard, Father Elias?'

Elias looked at him angrily. How could the doctor ask him that, when the boy was dying and Farre was to be his father?

'What are you saying!' he exclaimed. 'Why do you ask me a question like that?'

'But aren't these questions worldly men ask each other? Or aren't you a worldly man?'

Ah, yes. He was a wordly man, too! Unfortunately he still was, and as such he felt the bite of sorrow, spitefulness and jealousy.

Towards evening he returned to Maddalena and found her despairing because the boy's condition was growing worse. She was in the kitchen preparing something by the *focolare*.

'Mamma's there?' Elias asked, going towards the little room where the boy was lying.

'Yes.'

He would have liked to ask if Farre was also there, but he couldn't. Elias felt that *he* was there, sitting near the little bed; he saw distinctly the large body, he heard his panting breath; and he felt an almost morbid anguish. And yet when he opened the door and saw Farre sitting near the little bed, his heavy body a little bent over, silent, panting, Elias jumped as though frightened by the sudden apparition.

'The boy is dying, and he is there and won't let me come near, won't let me see him or touch him!' he thought bitterly. In fact, he kept a distance from the foot of the bed and looked almost shyly at the sick little boy.

'He's bad, he's bad,' Farre said sorrowfully, as though talking to himself.

Elias stayed a moment, then he went away without a word. He had a terrible night, and early the next morning he was there again. As he crossed the lane he imagined he'd find the boy improved, and his face lit up with hope. He entered, with a light step he crossed the courtyard and the kitchen and pushed the door open. And soon his face turned ashen. Farre was there again, sitting next to the boy's little bed, his plump body bending forward, silent, panting.

Maddalena was crying. As soon as she saw Elias she came towards him, drying her tears on her apron, and, repressing her sobs, told him the boy was dying. Elias looked at her despairingly from head to toe; he made no move towards her, he didn't speak; and shortly he left the room.

Zia Annedda followed him into the kitchen, then into the courtyard and asked him hesitantly: 'Elias, my son, what's wrong? Are you ill, too?'

He stopped near the door, turned, and bitter words against Farre and Maddalena, who let her fiancé always stay by the little sick one, came to his lips. But when he saw his mother's face, so pale and anguished, he murmured: 'No, I'm all right.' And he went away.

'What did he say? I didn't hear him,' Zia Annedda said to herself. 'Is he sick, too? What's wrong with him? Help us, *Santa Franziscu meu*!'

From that moment a real obsession had Elias in its grip. Whenever he was free he invariably went, almost without realizing it, to his house. Even before coming down the lane he felt that Farre was there in his place; nevertheless he continued to hope the contrary and would go in. And the hateful figure was there, always there.

187

Gradually he was seized by a kind of delirium. It came with the desire to bend over the child, to kiss him, to cure him with his hands, to say loving things to him. He felt that the strength of his love would be enough to cure him; and instead, as soon as he saw Farre, it was enough to make him feel paralysed; he didn't even dare put his hand on the dying boy's forehead, while inside he howled with pain and rage.

The evening of the seventh day of Berte's illness, Zia Annedda met him in tears.

'He won't get through the night,' she murmured.

'Is Farre still there, mamma?'

'No, he isn't.'

He rushed into the little room, pushed aside Maddalena who was crying silently beside the little bed, and bent anxiously over the boy. He was dying; his little face, once so full and pleasing, was ashen, thin, marked by agonizing suffering. It seemed like the face of a moribund little old man.

Elias didn't dare touch him or kiss him, caught by a sudden stupor. Just as before his brother Pietro's body, he had a vision of death, and realized that until that moment it had been impossible that Berte should die. But he was dying. Why? How? What was death? The end of everything, every passion? And why did he hate Farre? Why was he suffering?

'My son, my little son,' he moaned to himself. 'You are dying and I haven't loved you; instead of loving you, caring for you, keeping you from death, I've been lost in vain hatred, in vain jealousy . . . And now it's all

188

over, and there's no more time, there's no more time
for anything . . .'

A sudden desire seized him to take the little one in
his arms, to carry him away, save him. Save him?
How? He didn't know, but it seemed to him that it was
enough to put out his arms, to lean his body over the
boy's little body to hold death off. At that point Farre
entered and came slowly to the bed. Elias heard his
heavy step, his panting breathing, and instinctively
moved away.

Farre took his place; and once again Elias felt an
insurmountable obstacle between himself and the soul
of his boy. He went to the back of the room, near the
little window and his eyes flashed with a dark green
gleam. He was thinking deliriously: 'Why is he there?
Why did he take me away from there? He has chased
me, pushed me away. By what right? Is this boy his or
mine? He's mine, he's mine, not his! Now I'm going,
I'll box his ears, that fat windbag, I'll chase him away
from there, because I should stay there, and not he.
I'm going, I'm going, I'm going to hit him, kill him. I
want to drink his blood because I hate him, because
he's taken everything, everything, everything away
from me, because when he's here I start wanting my
boy to die.'

But for some minutes he didn't move from his place;
then he went back into the kitchen and said to his
mother: 'I'll be back in a little while,' and he went
rapidly out.

Going back into his cell, he seemed to awaken from
a dream; and he was aware of his life, of his state, and

of his duty. He knelt and began to pray, asking God's pardon for his frenzy.

'Pardon me, Lord, pardon me for eternal life, since I'm not worthy of pardon in this one. I'll never rest; I'm damned to suffer, but every punishment is small compared to the offence I've committed. Yes, yes, make me suffer as I deserve, but give me the strength to do my duties, take every vain passion from my heart. I'll promise to do everything to conquer myself. If the boy lives I'll come to see him as little as possible. Is he mine? No. I have nothing in this world; no children, no relatives, no goods, no passions. I must be alone; alone before you, my God, great and merciful Lord.'

But an hour later they advised him to return home in a hurry; he ran, pale and with a tumultuous heart. It was night; an autumn night, veiled, silent. The moon swam slowly among tenuous vapours, surrounded by an immense dull gold halo; a profound silence, an arcane and sad peace, something mysterious was in the air.

Elias sensed that the boy was dead, and entering the kitchen he saw, in fact, that Maddalena was sitting next to the *focolare* weeping tragically, taking her head in her hands from time to time. She was like a slave from whom everything had been taken – freedom, country, idols, family.

Elias felt the woman's immense sorrow, and thought: 'At this moment perhaps she believes that the loss of the boy is punishment for her sin; and she doesn't know that from this sorrow she'll come out purified and that she'll find the right way. The ways of the Lord are great, they are infinite!' While he was thinking in this way, he was looking around the semi-dark kitchen and didn't see Farre among those gathered there. Painfully he realized that the man was still there, near the dead child.

He went in. Farre wasn't there. Only Zia Annedda, very pale but calm, without crying, without making any sound, was washing and dressing the little dead child. Elias gave her some help. From the chest he took the boy's little stockings and shoes, and putting them on he felt that the colourless feet, shrunken by the illness, were still soft and warm.

When the little body was dressed and arranged on the pillows, and while Zia Annedda was there, Elias kept calm, but as soon as he was alone he felt a shudder go through his body, he felt his face and hands grow cold, and he knelt and hid his face in the cover of the little bed.

At last, at last, he was alone with his boy; no one could ever take him away, no one could ever come between them. And in his infinite grief he felt a tenuous veil of peace, almost of joy settle over him – like the haze of that mysterious autumn night – because his soul was alone at last before the great and merciful Lord, purified by sorrow, alone and free of every human passion.

Notes

The entries in quotation marks come from Grazia Deledda's 'Tradizioni popolari di Nuoro', first published in *Rivista delle Tradizioni Popolari Italiane* (Rome, 1894), edited by Angelo de Gubernatis (reprint edn., Cagliari, 1972).

1. 'In many Sardinian towns a special bread [*carta di musica*] was used that lasted many weeks without spoiling.'

2. 'Men's shirts, called *ghentones*, are very short, reaching slightly below the waist. They are usually made of strong linen . . . embroidered. The jacket is scarlet . . . Instead of an overcoat many shepherds wear skins that are long jackets without sleeves.' (p. 119)

3. 'When someone is freed from prison he is wished "Another one hundred years from now." The response to every good wish is "God willing!" ' (p. 105)

4. 'Sardinians call chickens with *più, più,* and cats with *musci, musci.* And dogs *te, te.*' (p. 16)

5. '[The Nuorese] loves wine; little matter if his bread is made of barley and his trencher lacks meat; however, wine is indispensable to him.' (p. 10)

6. 'Women visitors are served coffee . . . and the men wine. Nuorese women, and almost all Sardinian women, consider it shameful to drink wine in public, though they greatly abuse coffee.' (p. 102)

7. Grazia Deledda is writing from first-hand experience; she wrote letters to important people and did all she could for her brother Andrea when he was convicted of chicken stealing.

8. 'In Sardinia human justice . . . is more feared than divine justice.' (p. 12)

9. 'The books preferred by the farmers and shepherds who know how to read are the *Reali di Francia, Guerino detto Mechino, Bertoldo* and some other adventure books.' (p. 111)

10. 'Every little bush has ears' – a Sardinian proverb.

11. A magical incantation, often made by candle-light.

12. 'The characteristic carnival costume in Nuoro is

the 'Turk'. The trousers are made by securing a long white shirt at the ankles. A woman's jacket and corset are worn backwards, that is, fastened at the back, and a brightly coloured silk scarf is wrapped around the head, giving the illusion of an oriental costume.' (p. 120)

13. 'Up close this song is really not very pleasant. The tenors cover the singer's voice, and except for the first verse they are difficult to hear. But from a distance, it has such a sad, melancholy, serious, and desolate melody, that every time I hear it I think involuntarily of the wild landscape of the Nuorese area, desolate plains and marshes and rock peaks tinted pink by the solitary sunset. There is all the mysterious melancholy of a sad people, isolated, lost in vast country silence, an indistinct memory of savage life, a sad, indefinable hope.' (p. 111)

14. According to Deledda, 'Mourning is a terrible thing in Nuoro.' All the doors and windows are closed and the fires put out. The condolences of friends and relatives last for three days. 'Mourning varies from seven to eight years for a father to two years – the minimum – for a distant relative.' (pp. 102–3)

15. It was an old custom for men to get together and drink wine and make up verses on the spot.

EUROPEAN CLASSICS

Honoré de Balzac	*The Bureaucrats*
Heinrich Böll	*Absent without Leave*
	And Never Said a Word
	And Where Were You, Adam?
	The Bread of Those Early Years
	End of a Mission
	Irish Journal
	Missing Persons and Other Essays
	A Soldier's Legacy
	The Train Was on Time
	Women in a River Landscape
Madeleine Bourdouxhe	*La Femme de Gilles*
Lydia Chukovskaya	*Sofia Petrovna*
Grazia Deledda	*After the Divorce*
	Elias Portolu
Aleksandr Druzhinin	*Polinka Saks • The Story of Aleksei Dmitrich*
Venedikt Erofeev	*Moscow to the End of the Line*
Konstantin Fedin	*Cities and Years*
Fyodor Vasilievich Gladkov	*Cement*
I. Grekova	*The Ship of Widows*
Marek Hlasko	*The Eighth Day of the Week*
Bohumil Hrabal	*Closely Watched Trains*
Erich Kästner	*Fabian: The Story of a Moralist*
Ignacy Krasicki	*The Adventures of Mr. Nicholas Wisdom*
Miroslav Krleža	*The Return of Philip Latinowicz*
Karin Michaëlis	*The Dangerous Age*
Andrey Platonov	*The Foundation Pit*
Arthur Schnitzler	*The Road to the Open*
Ludvík Vaculík	*The Axe*
Vladimir Voinovich	*The Life & Extraordinary Adventures of Private Ivan Chonkin*
	Pretender to the Throne